A WITCH FOR MR. FROST

WITCHES OF CHRISTMAS GROVE
BOOK FIVE

DEANNA CHASE

Copyright © 2023 by Deanna Chase

Editing: Angie Ramey

Cover image: © Ravven

ISBN 978-1-953422-73-6

Bayou Moon Press, LLC

www.deannachase.com

Printed in the United States of America

ABOUT THIS BOOK

Welcome to Christmas Grove, the enchanted town full of love, magic, and holiday miracles.

Earth witch, Payton McCabe finally has her dream job in a town she loves. Christmas Grove is not only magical, but it has the small-town charm she's always craved. Love isn't on her radar. In fact, she's never wanted to get married. So, when she agrees to pretend to be a rock star's wife for a weekend, she figures she'll do her part to help him out and then it'll be over, right? Wrong. Now she's falling for a bad boy rock star and one way or another, she knows her heart is going to be broken.

Spirit witch, Atlas Mazer is on top of the world. As the front man for the bestselling rock band in recent years, he can't imagine settling down. But when his grandmother's health takes a turn for the worst, he's desperate to give her the one thing she's always wanted—to see him walk down the aisle. Now he's a groom in a fake wedding and falling for a woman who has only promised him a weekend. Will he find love this Christmas or will he be dateless on New Year's Eve... again?

CHAPTER 1

*P*ayton McCabe whirled around in the kitchen of The Enchanted and quickly stirred the chowder just in time to keep it from scorching. Her magic tingled, indicating the chowder was exactly right. Just as she was turning the burner off, not one, but two timers went off.

She went to open the bottom oven, but a pull in her gut told her the croissants in the top oven were going to burn if she didn't get to them first. On autopilot, trusting her witchy powers, she retrieved the croissants and then her famous cheesecake. Once she had all the timers turned off and everything cooling, she blew out a breath and leaned against the counter, pleased everything had turned out perfectly.

A slow clap sounded from the kitchen doorway that led into the lobby of the inn.

Payton rolled her eyes, and without looking back, she

said, "How about instead of mocking me, you get in here and help me with these dishes?"

"Is there a reason the inn hasn't hired a dishwasher?" a smoky voice asked.

"If you're going to criticize, then maybe it's time to start volunteering," she said, annoyed that some stranger was intruding on her kitchen. She finally turned around to see who was deliberately getting under her skin and froze. "Atlas Mazer? What are you doing here?"

"Awe, Payton, is that anyway to welcome your long-lost husband?" The rock star, dressed in tight jeans and a black long-sleeved Henley, was leaning against the doorjamb with his arms crossed over his well-defined chest, acting as if he hadn't just said something completely insane.

"Unless we got married in a drunken haze in Vegas, then I think you've got the wrong girl," Payton said, already turning her back to him. Atlas Mazer was a world-renowned, cocky rock star she'd met eleven months ago at Priscilla Cain and Leo West's wedding. He'd made a crazy proposal, asking her to be his pretend wife for a weekend in exchange for five hundred thousand dollars. She'd had just enough to drink that she'd thought, *Sure, I could do that,* and had agreed.

She hadn't been surprised when she'd never heard from him again. Clearly, he'd come to his senses and forgot all about whatever scheme he'd cooked up.

"No, that didn't happen. If it had, I'm sure it would've been in the gossip column for weeks. But I did secure a fake marriage certificate to prove we're hitched." He winked, and his lips curved up into a sexy half-smile.

"What?" she asked, staring at him like he'd lost his mind.

He pushed off the doorjamb and walked right into the kitchen as if he owned the place. When he stopped next to the counter, he stared into her eyes and said, "We need it to look official if we plan to fool anyone."

Payton tried to form words, but the man's presence was too overwhelming. She was lost in his smoldering turquoise eyes, and she felt herself flush as her pulse kicked into overdrive. Her hands twitched to touch him, and she had to take a step back just to get control of herself. What was happening? She'd never had such an intense physical response to a man before. She wanted to both throw herself at him and run from the kitchen.

"There's a family gathering this weekend," Atlas said. "It's at a private cabin on Silver Moon Lake. It's just my immediate family, so really, all you'll need to do is pretend to be in love with me for four days. But judging by your reaction to me, that shouldn't be a problem." He winked and reached for her hand.

"What are you doing?" Payton asked as she stared in utter shock at the giant diamond solitaire he was slipping onto the ring finger of her left hand.

"My grandmother isn't going to buy that I married you if you aren't wearing a ring. Come on, Payton, keep up. Think of it as a bonus on top of the 500k I'm giving you. Not a bad payday for a long weekend, right?"

"Okay, hold up." Payton threw her hands up and couldn't help staring at the giant rock on her finger when it caught the light. After a moment, she blinked and then shook her head, forcing herself to snap out of it. She met Atlas's amused gaze and scowled. "What makes you think you can waltz in here, put a ring on my finger, and then expect me to engage in some crazy scheme where you'd be lying to your grandmother?"

He raised both eyebrows. "Because I'm paying you and you already agreed to it?"

"That was on New Year's Eve last year, Mr. Rock Star. Do you really think I was just waiting around here for you to drop in and collect on my drunken promise?"

"No, but I imagine you thought about it a time or two," he said with a wry smile. "It's not every day you get to play wife to a rock star and make a tidy little nest egg for just four days of work."

The man had a point, but there was no way Payton was going to admit that he was right. She knew exactly what she'd do with that money. She'd pay off the loan she took out to invest in her brother's restaurant, and then she'd use the rest to open her own business.

There was a storefront in downtown Christmas Grove that was perfect for the pie store she'd been dreaming of opening. Christmas Grove was known for its plethora of berries as well as it's apple groves. Since she'd become the head chef at The Enchanted, the charming inn run by her friend Olivia Mann, her pies had quickly become a specialty. She'd stopped counting how many people had asked how they could buy whole pies to take home. Without a shop where she could make them in volume, selling them was just impossible. But with the money he was offering, she could make her pies in the morning, hire someone to man the shop, and still oversee the kitchen at the inn. It would be a lot of work, but it was work she loved.

Atlas chuckled softly.

"Why are you laughing?" she asked, narrowing her eyes at him.

"Because, Payton McCabe, I recognize that spark of interest in your eyes. You might be annoyed at me, you might even be slightly insulted, but there's no denying that you want to do this. Whatever just put that look on your face, you want it badly. We both know it's worth four days of your time. Tell me I'm wrong."

"You're wrong," she said, folding her arms over her chest and trying to ignore the ache in her gut that told her she'd be crazy to pass up such a golden opportunity. "Even if I wanted to, I can't. I have to work." She waved a hand around the kitchen. "Someone has to cook for the guests."

He frowned as his brow furrowed. "Can't you find someone to fill in? It's just—"

"Four days, I know. I heard you the first time," she admonished. "And no, there isn't just someone who can fill in. Everyone works around here, Atlas. My assistant chef is out of town this weekend, and the only other person I'd trust is my brother. But he has his own restaurant to deal with. So I guess you're out of luck."

He pursed his lips as he studied her. "So you're saying that *if* someone could fill in, you'd do this? You'd come to the lake with me and pretend to be my new wife?"

Payton let out a long breath and shrugged. "My answer doesn't matter. It's just not going to happen." She waved a hand at the door. "Now go on. I have work to do."

He nodded once and disappeared from the kitchen. Payton stared after him, wondering what kind of person lied to their grandmother about being married. And why had she ever agreed to it in the first place? She knew why. That night, eleven months ago, she'd had just enough wine that her guard was completely down. And when the drop-dead-gorgeous man had flirted with her and offered her a ridiculous amount of money, she'd just gone with it.

But now, months later and sober in the light of day, she couldn't imagine engaging in any sort of scheme with the man. Not for any amount of money. No matter how tempting it might be.

She returned to her croissants and started placing them on the cooling rack. Her mind was racing with everything she had to get done before the dinner service started. There were sauces to make, green beans to blanche, and steaks to marinate.

Payton was busy mincing garlic when Atlas entered the kitchen again. Her hand tightened around the knife as she pressed her lips together in a thin line. Swallowing her annoyance, she forced herself to keep her tone neutral when she said, "I know you're used to getting everything you want when you want it, but my answer is still no." She pointed at the door with her knife. "Kindly step out of the kitchen before Olivia sees you. It's off-limits to guests and visitors."

Someone behind Atlas cleared their throat.

"Seriously? You brought someone else?" Payton asked, completely exasperated. "Atlas, this is unacceptable. I—"

"It's me," Olivia said, peeking out from behind the larger-than-life rock star.

Payton glanced between Atlas and her boss and then finally let her gaze land on Olivia. "I'm sorry. I didn't invite him here."

"I know. He explained everything just now." Olivia walked around Atlas and came to stand next to Payton. She placed a hand on Payton's arm and beamed at her. "We've worked it out so that you can have the weekend off."

"What?" Payton's heart sped up in a mild panic as she glanced between them. Atlas flashed that self-satisfied smile she desperately wanted to wipe off his face. Closing her eyes for a moment, she shook her head and then turned to her boss. Olivia's eyes were lit with excitement. "This isn't necessary, Olivia. I know you're trying to help, but I'm not going to pretend to be someone's wife, even if he does want to pay me an obscene amount of money. It's just not okay to lie to one's grandmother."

Olivia blinked at her before squeezing her hand. "Is it really so terrible, Pay? He's just trying to fulfill his grandmother's final wish to see him married and happy before she leaves this Earth."

"Your grandmother is dying?" Payton asked Atlas, studying him now.

All the cockiness had left him, and worry lines had formed on his forehead. He nodded once and glanced away before adding, "She's my favorite person in the whole world." Then he met Payton's eyes again and said, "I just want to give her this final gift. I know it's a lot to ask, but if you—"

"I'll do it." Payton's heart nearly broke at the pain she saw on Atlas's handsome face, and the words just flew out of her mouth before she could think too hard about the ramifications.

"You will?" he asked, sounding surprised.

"Yeah." Payton ran a hand through her hair. "You said four days, right? When do I need to be ready?"

He let out a long breath and the tension in his shoulders eased. Payton watched in fascination as that cocky mask slid over his face once more. "Four days," he confirmed. "I'll pick you up at your place Thursday at 9:00 a.m."

Payton and Olivia watched as the man disappeared from the kitchen. It was only when he was gone that Payton wondered exactly how he knew where she lived.

CHAPTER 2

"*A*re you going to sign that?" Declan asked as he lounged on Payton's couch with his feet propped up on the coffee table and one ankle crossed over the other. It was Wednesday evening, the night before the big weekend, and Payton still hadn't legally committed to her role as Atlas's fake wife.

Payton glanced at the pen in her right hand before placing it on the contract she'd just read for the third time. "Not until I read it one more time."

Her brother chuckled. "It's just a simple contract and an NDA, Payton. You're not committing to having the man's child or anything."

She ground her teeth together and gave him a death glare. "You're not the one who has to pretend to be married to an egotistical man-child who thinks all he has to do is throw money at something to get his way."

Declan dropped his feet to the floor and leaned forward, clasping his hands together. His dirty blond hair was mussed, and he looked a little troubled. He opened his mouth to speak, but she put a hand up, stopping him.

"I don't need a lecture right now, Deck. Just... don't."

"I wasn't going to lecture you," he said softly. His tone was so sincere that she finally gave him her full attention.

She mimicked his pose and looked into his blue eyes that mirrored her own. "Okay then, what were you going to say?"

"Just that if you really don't want to do this, then you don't have to. Have your lawyer call his and tell him it's off. Money isn't everything."

Payton swallowed the lump in her throat. "It's not, but..."

When she didn't continue, he reached for her hand and squeezed it lightly. "But it definitely would go a long way to ease your anxiety, right? You could pay off your bills and still have a generous nest egg for the future."

"Yeah. It would." Payton sat back in her chair and let herself think about everything she'd been through in her life. Their parents had been a disaster. They'd spent all of Declan's and Payton's childhood fighting. There was never enough money for anything, and it had made both her and her brother cautious with their finances.

"That would be really nice," Declan said with a sigh as he averted his gaze.

Payton narrowed her eyes at her brother and knew instantly there was something he wasn't telling her. "Deck? What's going on?"

"Nothing," he said too quickly, still not meeting her gaze. "It would just be nice to have a cushion. That's all."

She stood and walked over to her brother, staring down at him. She placed her hands on her hips and fixed him with a piercing stare. "Declan McCabe, spit it out. Are you having money problems? Is it the restaurant?"

He visibly swallowed and then reluctantly met her gaze as he nodded.

"But how?" she demanded. "I just went over the financials last week. We're right on target with our estimates and projections. What went wrong?"

He grimaced and looked like he was going to vomit.

"Okay, now you're really scaring me. Just tell me what happened." She couldn't imagine what the problem could be. Apollo's, the restaurant they co-owned, had just opened the month before, and so far everything had gone as smoothly as once could expect with a new restaurant. Sure, there'd been a few bumps in the road, but nothing catastrophic. Only a couple of staffing changes.

"It's Matisse," Declan said. "He called this afternoon. His business is on the verge of bankruptcy, and since he's an investor in our restaurant, it will be up for grabs when he goes into receivership. If we don't come up with the funds to buy him out by the first of the year, we're probably going to have to close." Matisse was Declan's former boss. He had restaurants in Napa and San Francisco. Without his investment in Apollo's, they wouldn't have been able to get it off the ground.

Payton's heart was in her throat. "We don't have that

kind of money. The restaurant isn't even turning a profit yet."

"I know," he said.

They'd committed to a big marketing push, and all the proceeds they were bringing in currently were slotted to go right back into the business. Payton pressed a hand to her heart. "Maybe we can get a loan to buy him out?"

Declan shook his head. "I can't. With the loan I took out to buy the property, I'm already maxed out."

Payton considered grabbing her laptop and doing some quick calculations, but she knew it would be a wasted effort. She'd barely qualified for the business loan she'd taken out for Apollo's earlier in the year. None of her financials had changed. There was no reason to believe a bank was going to loan her more money. She glanced at the NDA and contract sitting on the table.

"I didn't want to tell you while you were still thinking things over," Declan said.

She just nodded. Her brother was like that. He wouldn't want her to feel forced to make any decisions. "I'm glad you did." She sat down in the chair, grabbed the pen, and then quickly signed the paperwork. "There. It's done. By early next week, we'll have the money we need to keep our restaurant."

Silence filled her living room.

Finally Declan cleared his throat and said, "I hate that you feel like you had to do that."

"I know." She gave him a ghost of a smile. "It's just four days, right? What could possibly go wrong?"

They stared at each other and then as if on cue, they both groaned.

"You know you just cursed yourself, right?" Declan said.

"Ugh, don't say cursed. That sounds so… evil."

"Jinxed?" he asked.

"That's not much better, but I'll take it." She stood. "I'd better go pack. Atlas said he'd be here first thing in the morning." Payton took two steps, paused, and glanced back at her brother. "What does one wear to a family reunion with a rock star?"

"Faux fur and diamonds?" he suggested with a wink.

She laughed. "He's going to have to settle for fleece and sterling silver."

Declan rose from the couch and walked over to her, holding his arms out.

Payton stepped into his arms and hugged him with everything she had. He was everything to her, and now that she knew the restaurant that had been his dream for years was on the line, she'd do everything in her power to save it. Even if it meant lying to Atlas's grandmother. "I love you, big brother."

"Love you, too, Pay." He squeezed her tightly, and when he let her go, he grinned and said, "Don't forget the condoms."

She rolled her eyes and lightly punched him in the arm. "Are you implying I'm a prostitute?"

He blinked and took a step back. "Hell, no. Christmas on a cracker, Payton. I'd never imply that. I was just remembering how you looked at him last year at the wedding."

"And how was that?" she asked, cocking one eyebrow.

He chuckled. "Let's just say it was slightly X-rated." Before she could respond, he yanked the front door open and disappeared into the cool night air.

CHAPTER 3

*a*tlas pulled his Range Rover to a stop in front of the pretty yellow house and killed the engine. Instead of hopping out, he took a long moment to just breathe. He'd spent the week trying to mentally prepare for the long weekend. He knew in his heart that it was likely the last time he'd get to spend any significant time with his grandmother, and it was breaking him.

Her heart was giving out. The doctors and healers had repeatedly told him that there was nothing more they could do, and all the money in the world wasn't going to change things. He'd known this day was coming for over a year. It was why he'd propositioned Payton all those months ago, but as fate would have it, his grandmother had gotten better... for a while.

Then things took a turn for the worse.

With nothing else to do to improve her health, he was

giving her the one thing she'd always wanted—for him to be settled down with the love of his life.

Too bad it was a lie.

But she wouldn't know that. He'd make sure of it. If there was one thing that Atlas Mazer was good at, it was putting on a show. And that's exactly what Georgia Frost was going to get. The performance of a lifetime.

Having second thoughts?

"Why do you always pop in at the most inopportune moments?" Atlas asked the ghost of his twin brother.

I only show up when you need me. He grinned that same cocky smile Atlas had seen in the mirror thousands of times before. *It just so happens that you need me a lot more than you care to admit.*

That was true. Ashton, his twin and best friend in the entire world, had died in a car accident when they'd been out on their first tour together. Atlas had stayed back at the hotel to work out a vocal while his brother had gone out with a couple of the roadies to have a few beers. They'd never even made it to the pub. A truck T-boned them, and Ashton died instantly.

When Atlas got the news about his twin's accident, he'd nearly self-destructed. He'd canceled the tour and holed up for weeks in the house they'd shared. But then Ashton had appeared in his current form and demanded that his brother get his shit together. He'd insisted that Atlas get back in the studio and fulfill their dreams for both of them. Ever since that day, Ashton always showed up when Atlas needed him. It wasn't a surprise he was here now. Not when their grandmother was on her final days.

"Are you here for moral support or to tell me I'm acting crazy?" Atlas asked.

Why not both? Ashton's expression was a weird mix of sympathy and amusement.

"So you don't think I'm insane for doing this?"

No. His brother shook his head. *You're just trying to give Gigi a final gift. That's understandable. It's just that... I think you should be careful here.*

"I know. It's risky. But it's only four days. We should be able to keep up the charade long enough that we don't upset Gigi."

It's not her I'm worried about, Alistair.

Alistair. His brother and his grandmother were the only two people on earth who refused to call him by his adopted stage name he'd taken after Ashton's death. "Then who?"

You. He pointed at Atlas's heart. *I fear you're going to get in too deep this time around.*

Atlas frowned. "What's that supposed to mean?"

Just be careful you don't mess it up. Ashton gave him a cheeky smile and then faded back into the ether.

"Dammit." He hated when his brother gave him warnings. He'd learned long ago that more often than not, Ashton was right. It was annoying as hell to have a know-it-all ghost who followed him around. Especially since that ghost was his twin.

Atlas took a moment to put his game face on, and then once he was armored with his signature confidence, he climbed out of the SUV and made his way up the walkway. Before he even knocked, the door swung open and Payton walked out onto her porch. She had a manilla envelope in one hand and was dragging her suitcase behind her with the other.

"It's about time," she said, walking past him. "You sat in your vehicle so long I was starting to think you were having second thoughts."

Atlas stared after the pretty blonde, both amused and a little taken aback. Earlier in the week when he'd gone to the inn, she'd been so hesitant that he was half-expecting her to try to back out again. Especially since his lawyer had said they hadn't received the signed contracts yet.

Payton tugged on the back door of the Range Rover. When it didn't open, she turned back to look at Atlas with both eyebrows raised. "Well, rocker boy, are we going to do this or not?"

"We're doing this," he said and strode quickly to her side. After he unlocked the cargo door, he handled loading her luggage and then opened the passenger side door for her.

"Very gentlemanly," she said as though she were surprised that he wasn't a total heathen. Well, what had he expected? He'd sprung this weekend on her four days ago and hadn't been willing to take no for an answer. It was no surprise she didn't have the best opinion of him. It was something he was going to have to change sooner rather than later, because the last thing he needed was for her to be irritated with him in front of his grandmother.

"I think you'll find that I'm usually very chivalrous," he said.

She snorted, climbed into the passenger seat, and then buckled her seat belt as he pushed the door closed.

Atlas couldn't help himself. He laughed. How could he

not? She was the most amusing woman he'd met in years. Still chuckling to himself, he shook his head and walked around the vehicle. Once he was in the driver's seat, Payton waved the folder at him.

"The paperwork is signed. Now what?" she asked.

He glanced over at her. "Did you give a copy to your lawyer?"

"Of course." She rolled her eyes. "I'm not an idiot."

"I never said you were." He reached out for the folder and then tucked it behind the seat. "I'll have this messengered to my manager when we get to the cabin. She'll handle the rest."

Payton frowned at him.

"What?"

"Nothing. I…" She shook her head.

"Payton," he said, eyeing her. "You obviously want to ask me something. What is it?"

She glanced away for a moment but then straightened her spine as she turned to him. "The money you're paying me for this is time sensitive. I'm going to need it before the first of the year, and I just want to make sure your people aren't going to drag their feet when this is over."

"You already made plans for the money?" he asked, wondering why he was surprised. He knew she wasn't doing him this favor out of the goodness of her heart.

"Not plans exactly," she said hesitantly. "More like an unexpected expense came up, and it's important it gets taken care of as soon as possible."

He nodded. "I understand. Don't worry. As long as you stick out the weekend and don't let on that we aren't actually married, then the funds will be deposited into your bank account next week."

Payton let out a long breath and relaxed against the seat. "Okay. Well then, I guess we'd better get our story straight. Tell me, Atlas, how exactly did you make me fall in love with you?"

"With my music, obviously," he said with a wink.

"Oh come on. How cliché is that?" she asked, giving him a look of disappointment. "You can do better than that."

Atlas felt a tug of interest. If he hadn't just hired her to do a job, he had no doubt he'd be asking her to join him for dinner, or maybe a long weekend on a tropical island. He couldn't deny he loved a challenge. And Payton McCabe clearly wasn't going to give him a moment's peace. "All right. We first met at Priscilla's wedding, and when I asked you to dance, you turned me down. So I made it my mission to charm you until you granted me a spin on the dance floor. But I didn't know until the end of the night that the reason you turned me down was because of your broken leg. All along, I thought I was charming you, but the truth was you were charming me. I knew then and there you were the one for me."

Payton just blinked at him.

"Not good enough?" he asked, disappointed. He'd thought he'd come up with a slam dunk.

"No. It's good enough," she said, sounding a little awed. "I just wasn't expecting... that."

"Expecting what?" he asked with a curious chuckle. "What do you mean by 'that'?"

"I don't know." She smiled to herself, shaking her head.

"I'm just surprised that you'd make it sound so sweet, I guess. I figured you were so used to women falling at your feet that you'd say I was the one pursuing you."

"Nah. Gigi would never believe I fell for a woman who was chasing me. She knows me better than that."

"So you like the chase; is that it?" she asked, curiosity sparking in her pale blue eyes.

Atlas turned down a narrow driveway that was lined heavily with pine trees. Though it was a sunny day, there was still snow clinging to the needles. He didn't say anything until a few moments later when he pulled to a stop in front of a sprawling mountain cabin. Then he turned to her and said, "I used to. But I gave that up years ago... until now."

CHAPTER 4

*a*tlas was out of the Range Rover before Payton could ask him what the hell he meant by that. Who exactly was he chasing? Her? She shook her head. That wasn't right. He pulled her door open and offered his hand.

Payton let him help her out of the SUV, and as soon as her feet hit the ground, she was just on the verge of demanding an answer when the front door opened and a stream of people rushed out.

"Atlas!" an older woman called and ran to him, throwing her arms around him.

He tightened his grip on Payton's hand and hugged the woman with one arm. "Aunt Patty, it's been too long."

The bottle redhead pulled back and grinned up at him. "I'm so glad we have you for the weekend."

"Me, too." He glanced at Payton. "Aunt Patty, I want you to meet my wife, Payton."

Wife. The word was like a sucker punch to the gut. She'd

thought she'd made peace with her decision when she'd signed the paperwork, but she hadn't anticipated feeling like such a fraud the moment she had to go through with their charade.

"Oh, honey. Don't be scared. None of us bite," Patty said with a kind smile. Then she glanced over her shoulder at a tall man who looked a lot like Atlas. "Well, most of us anyway. Keep an eye on Danny. He's had a feisty streak ever since he could walk."

The man she'd referred to as Danny just shook his head. "Funny, Mom. Doesn't that ever get old?"

She turned to him and patted his cheek. "No, sweetheart. It's my revenge for that time you bit me when you were three years old. Deal with it."

Danny grimaced and looked at Payton. "Maybe you could pretend you didn't hear any of that?"

"Uh, sure," Payton said.

Atlas pulled her in close to him and wrapped an arm around her waist. "Maybe we could put the crazy away until Payton gets to know everyone a little bit. We don't want to scare her off in the first ten minutes, do we?"

"If this is enough to scare her off, I think you have work to do, buddy," Danny said, clapping Atlas on the back and chuckling.

"I'm not scared," Payton said, pasting on a smile and leaning into Atlas. If she was going to do this, she might as well start acting like the devoted wife, right?

"That's what we like to hear," a tall blonde said, coming over and hugging them both. After she let go, she held her hand out to Payton. "I'm Alison, Atlas's favorite sister."

"Only sister," he said.

"I'm still his favorite," she said cheekily and pulled Payton out of his arms. "Come on. Let's go in and get you settled. No need for the entire family to mob you all at once."

Payton glanced back at Atlas, desperately wishing she wasn't being whisked away. What if Alison asked her something she couldn't answer? It wasn't like they'd ironed out a full story to tell about their courtship. She'd just have to be as vague as possible until they could talk again.

"Okay. Tell me everything," Alison said as soon as they walked into the house.

Payton heard her but didn't respond as she stared in awe at the beautiful home.

The *cabin* wasn't like any cabin she'd ever seen before. The foyer was a grand space with a twenty-foot ceiling. To the left was a hallway that seemed to go on forever. To the right was a gorgeous kitchen with sage green cabinets and white marble countertops. Payton could tell even from a distance that every appliance was top of the line. But straight ahead was the showstopper, a great room that was lined with floor-to-ceiling windows that looked out over the sparkling blue waters of Silver Moon Lake.

"This place is fantastic," she breathed to Alison.

"Isn't it? Atlas arranged it for the family." She guided Payton all the way to the end of the hall, past a number of bedrooms, another family room, and what appeared to be a media room, before they finally stopped at a massive bedroom. It was sort of isolated from the rest of the house, giving it an air of privacy.

"This can't be my room," Payton said as her eyes nearly bugged out when she spotted the en suite bathroom that looked as if it had been taken directly from the pages of *Architectural Digest*.

Alison furrowed her brow. "Is there something wrong with it?"

"What?" Payton spun to look at her. "No. Not at all. It's just so... fancy."

Atlas's sister chuckled and shook her head, looking at Payton as if she'd just said something ridiculous. "Oh, Payton. I'd think you'd be used to the opulence by now. Atlas doesn't do anything halfway." She pumped her eyebrows suggestively. "Besides, with you two being newlyweds, it's probably better your room has a buffer from the rest of us."

"Right," Payton said, feeling like an idiot. It hadn't even occurred to her that she'd be expected to share a room with Atlas. What exactly had she been thinking? That their family consisted of a bunch of monks? Even if they weren't pretending to be married, it was likely they'd expect Atlas to be sleeping with whomever he brought to the family gathering. "I guess I'm still adjusting."

"You'll get there." Alison leaned over and gave her a kiss on her cheek. "Go ahead and get settled in. We have a big day ahead of us."

Before Payton could ask what that meant, Alison was gone.

Payton stood in the gorgeous room, knowing she should unpack her bag. But her gaze landed on the eastern view of the lake, and the next thing she knew she was sinking into one of the oversized chairs and curling up to take it all in. With the mountains in the background and the sun sparkling on the water, a sense of complete peace washed over her. She didn't care about the opulence of the house. But the view... It was everything. She could have happily stayed right where she was for the rest of the day.

"Hey, babe," Atlas said softly.

Payton jumped and spun in the chair to stare at the man who was crouched right next to her and smiling like a fool. "You think that's funny? Sneaking up on me like that?"

He shrugged. "Yes."

"And don't call me babe. It's weird," she said.

Atlas moved to sit in the chair next to her. "It's probably best you get used to it, cause it's what I'm going to call you in front of my family."

She groaned. "Do you have to?"

"Yes." He stood and held out his hand. "Come on, babe. It's time to meet the matriarch."

"Now?"

"Yes. She's waiting." He took her hand and gently tugged her to her feet. "Don't worry. Gigi is the best."

"But we haven't worked out our wedding details. All I know is that we met on New Year's Eve." Panic had taken over, and Payton was sure she'd never be able to pull this off.

"Relax, Pay," he said, moving toward the door. "I've got this."

"Famous last words."

He snorted out a soft laugh, kept her hand in his, and led the way back to the main living space.

"Alistair," an older woman said, her voice a little shaky as she opened her arms, welcoming Atlas. "It's so good to see you."

Atlas dropped Payton's hand and went to the woman, giving her a hug. She clung to him, holding on for a long moment.

When they finally broke apart, Atlas reached for Payton's hand again and pulled her to him. "Gigi, I want you to meet my wife, Payton. Payton, my beloved grandmother, Georgia Frost."

Gigi held her arms open for Payton. And then again, just like she'd done with Atlas, Gigi held on tightly as if she never wanted to let go. "I'm so happy to welcome you to the family. If Alistair loves you, then I know I will, too."

Payton felt a pang of guilt. How could they be lying to this sweet woman? But then she remembered that Atlas was just trying to give her one last gift, and she decided that maybe the motivation justified the deception.

When Gigi finally let go, Payton couldn't help but notice the tears glistening in the older woman's eyes. Her heart squeezed, and suddenly she understood why Atlas was willing to go through such an elaborate plan just to please her.

"Sit. Both of you," Gigi said, waving to the couch that was next to her chair.

Atlas sank into the couch and pulled Payton down onto his lap.

Payton let out a startled laugh. "I think there's plenty of seating, *babe*." The word *babe* felt weird and unfamiliar coming from her lips.

"What's the fun in that?" he asked as he nuzzled her neck, putting on a full show for his grandmother.

"Aww, young love. I'm so happy to see you smitten, Ali."

"Gigi," he said, side-eyeing her, "you know how I feel about that nickname."

"I do. But you'll grin and bear it because it makes me happy," she said. Her watery blue eyes glinted with mischief, and Payton thought she was the cutest grandmother she'd ever met.

"Tell me everything," Gigi said. "How did you meet? And how long was it before you knew she was the one for you?" she asked Atlas.

"That's easy," Atlas said, giving Payton a sly grin. "We met on New Year's Eve, and I proposed that night. Love at first sight. Of course it took her months to agree, but here we are."

At least that much is true, Payton thought. It would make it easier not to get caught in a lie.

"When and where did you get married?" his grandmother asked. "It must have been super-secret if the tabloids didn't get wind of it."

"It was very low-key," he said with a nod. "Nothing fancy. Just us and a friend who got ordained on the internet. A backyard type of wedding. We wanted it just for us."

"That's really romantic, sweetheart," she said and then grew really quiet. "I just wish I'd been there."

"Me, too, Gigi," he said. "Me, too. But we're here now. Ready to celebrate with you and the rest of the family."

She nodded once, but then a pleased smile claimed her lips as she glanced past them.

Payton turned to see Alison standing behind them, holding a notebook and gesturing something to Gigi. When she spotted Payton watching her, she tucked the notebook behind her back and grinned.

"Are you guys ready to get your decorating on?" Alison asked. "Zach from the Christmas Tree farm is here with a massive tree."

"Oh, grand," Gigi said, her face lighting up with happiness. "It will be great to see him again."

"You know Zach?" Payton asked, feeling mildly panicked. No one except Declan and Olivia knew that Payton was playing Atlas's wife. If word got out, it'd be a media frenzy and a complete circus. She prayed that Zach wasn't the gossiping type.

"Oh, yes. He's family. Didn't you know?" Gigi asked.

"Zach is a third or fourth cousin," Alison said. "We share our great-great-grandfather Frost."

"Third cousin," Payton said automatically then gave Atlas a worried look.

He just shrugged, looking unconcerned like he always did. Did nothing ever bother the man? He seemed to act as if everything would work out. Who could blame him, really? It certainly looked like he lived a charmed life.

"Hello?" a man called from the foyer.

"Zach!" Alison hurried to him and spoke in a hushed whisper. They both turned to look at Payton and Atlas, making Payton feel even more self-conscious. But then Zach nodded once, and they started discussing where the tree would go.

"Are you close with Zach?" Payton asked Atlas.

"Not at all," he said. "In fact, I think I've only met him a couple of times. Once at a funeral and once at one of Gigi's extended family reunions."

"Zach's grandmother and I were very good friends," Gigi said. "We both married into the family the same month and even lived next door to each other for a couple of years. She was lovely." The older woman gazed past them, her eyes appearing unfocused as she seemed to get lost in her memories.

Atlas gestured for Payton to get up, and then together they went over to say hello to Zach.

"Hi, cuz," Atlas said, holding out his hand.

"Hey, Atlas. I hear congratulations are in order," Zach said, smiling at Payton.

Payton swallowed a groan. How was she going to explain her short-lived marriage to the town she'd adopted? Maybe this wasn't such a good idea.

No. This was going to save Declan's restaurant and her investment in it. All she had to do was just ignore any gossip and keep moving.

"Thanks, man. Have you met my wife, Payton?" Atlas asked.

"Sure." Zach turned to Payton and gave her a quick hug. "You let me know if he doesn't treat you right," Zach said with a cheeky grin. "I'll make sure he steps back into line."

"Thanks, Zach, but I think I can handle him," Payton said, trying to play along.

"I bet you can."

"Listen, Zach," Atlas said. "I was hoping you could keep our news to yourself for a while. We haven't announced anything to the press and would like time to ourselves before the media frenzy starts. You know how town gossip is—"

"Say no more," Zach said. "Alison already mentioned it, so I'll keep this under wraps."

"Thank you," Atlas said, giving him a quick bro hug.

"No problem." Zach crossed the room to talk to Gigi. She seemed to get a little misty-eyed as she clutched his hands in hers and asked him about his wife and family.

Atlas's Aunt Patty appeared with his Uncle Tim. After introductions were made, they, along with Alison and Atlas, worked out where they wanted the tree. Once Zach was done talking to Gigi, he retrieved the tree, and twenty minutes later it was situated near the window and ready to be decorated.

"Have fun this weekend," Zach said, waving to everyone as he headed for the door. "Let me know if you need anything else."

"We will!" Alison called to him. Then she turned and rubbed her hands together. "Okay, time to decorate."

"With what?" Payton asked. Surely the rental house didn't have decorations just sitting around.

"We brought the ornaments and decorations from Gigi's house," Alison said, grabbing Atlas. "Help me get the totes."

"I'll help," Payton said and followed along.

Once they pulled the totes from one of the SUVs in the driveway, the three of them gathered around the tree while the rest of the family sat waiting.

Atlas rummaged through a couple of the plastic totes until he found what he was looking for. "Ah-ha! Got it." He turned to Gigi and held up a beautiful blown glass ornament. "Ready, Gigi?"

She nodded.

Alison and Atlas flanked both sides of her and carefully helped her to her feet. She was shaky and so frail looking, but when she wrapped her hands around the glass ball, a soft, loving smile claimed her lips and there was no denying how much she treasured the ornament.

Atlas kept his arm wrapped around her, carefully holding her up as she reached to place the ornament prominently on the tree.

"It won't be long now, Edgar," she said, her eyes watery. "I hope you're ready for me."

"He and Pickles have been waiting patiently, Gigi," Atlas said. "But don't be in a hurry to leave the rest of us behind, okay? I'm not quite ready."

She turned to him and placed both hands on his cheeks. "I love you, Alistair Frost. Don't ever forget that."

"I won't," he choked out as tears shone in his dark turquoise eyes.

Gigi gently wiped away the one tear that fell to his cheek, and Payton found herself more than a little overwhelmed by the obvious love Atlas had for his grandmother. This wasn't a show. This was real love. It became clear that he'd do anything to make her happy. She vowed right then and there to do everything in her power to sell their fake marriage to Gigi that weekend.

"I'm tired. Alistair, can you help me to my room?" Gigi asked.

"Of course, gorgeous. Let's go."

Payton watched as Gigi clung to Atlas's arm, her head tilted toward him as she proceeded to tell him all about the day she met her love, Edgar. He was patient, prompting her when she seemed to lose her place in the story, and Payton had no doubt he'd heard the story numerous times already. She pressed her hand to her heart, blinked back tears, and wondered if anyone other than Gigi ever saw that side of Atlas Mazer.

CHAPTER 5

"*R*each. You got it, babe. Just a little further," Atlas urged Payton as she stretched to place the topper on the Christmas tree they'd just spent the last hour decorating. He held Payton at the waist, steadying her to keep her stable on the ladder.

"Almost there." She pressed up onto her tiptoes and placed the glass topper onto the tree. But the moment she let go, her foot slipped and she let out a startled cry.

Atlas quickly pulled her into his arms, cradling her against his chest. "Are you okay?"

"Yeah," she breathed, clutching his neck. "Thanks."

"You can fall into my arms anytime." He tightened his grip on her, holding her closer.

Danny shook his head and chuckled. "Well played, cuz."

Atlas and Danny quickly shared a fist bump, making Payton roll her eyes.

"Grooooan," Alison said, grinning as she teased them. "You're making me nauseous."

"That's the sushi you had for dinner last night," he said and then winked at Payton.

"Um, you can let me down now," she said.

"Nope." He shook his head, enjoying having her in his arms more than he should. Not only did he like the way she felt in his arms, but he was also eternally grateful for the effort she was putting into the weekend already. His grandmother had confided that she had already fallen in love with Payton. He had to agree. Not only had she agreed to help decorate the tree, but she'd also all but taken over and made sure to take special care with all of Gigi's favorite ornaments. Her empathy had touched him deeply.

"Atlas," she said softly.

"Yeah?"

"I'd like it if you put me down."

"Right." He carefully lowered her to her feet, and when she untangled herself from him, he immediately missed having her in his arms.

"Okay, who else wants lunch?" Payton asked, already heading to the kitchen. "Did anyone think to bring groceries?"

"The host stocked the kitchen for us, but I'm not at all sure what's in there," Alison said, hurrying to catch up with Payton.

Atlas pulled out his phone, already pulling up an app to order something, but when he opened it, he quickly learned there was no delivery at the house. If he wanted to order anything, someone would have to go pick it up. It wasn't ideal, since he didn't want to spend any time away from his grandmother this weekend, but it was better than making Payton scrounge through the kitchen. He scrolled through his phone, found an Italian place that looked decent, and headed into the kitchen.

"Hey, guys," he said, still scrolling through the options, wondering if they should pick up something for dinner as well. "We can just order something from town."

"Why would we do that?" Payton asked.

He glanced up and spotted her in an apron with a variety of ingredients on the island countertop. "Payton, it's your weekend off. You shouldn't have to cook."

"No one is forcing me," she said with a grin. "I want to. You know how I am if I don't spend enough time in the kitchen. I need my fix, or else I'm going to get cranky."

"I can't believe you married a chef, Atlas," Alison said, shaking her head. "I swear, your life is charmed. It's really annoying."

Payton laughed, her blue eyes sparkling so bright he found himself unable to look away from her.

"Earth to Atlas." Alison waved a hand in front of his face. "You do realize you're staring, don't you?"

He ignored his sister, but when his brother popped in, there was no pretending he wasn't there. The cheese that was on the counter rose into the air, followed by a package of gourmet salami.

Payton's eyebrows raised as she watched her ingredients dance across the kitchen. "Uh, Atlas? Is this place haunted?"

"Sort of," he said and then scowled at his brother. "Dude, put those down."

Do you have any idea what she's going to do with these? Ashton asked, eyeing both the cheese and salami as if he were going to tear right through the plastic packaging with his teeth.

"Apparently, she's making lunch," Atlas said.

Not just lunch, Alistair. Homemade pizza. His twin shook his head and then frowned before herding the missing ingredients back to the island counter. *If you don't lock this one down for real, I'll do it for you.*

"What? Do you think this is an episode of *Ghosts* or something?" Atlas accused his brother. "Don't even think about it. Understand?"

What are you going to do about it if I do? Ashton taunted. *It's not like I'm at all concerned about taking an ass-whooping.* He threw his head back and laughed as if that were the funniest thing he'd ever said.

Atlas crossed his arms over his chest and glared at his ghostly twin. "I could start burning some sage. How'd you like that?"

The two packages fell with a *thunk* onto the counter, and then Ashton turned, his body vibrating with... anger? Frustration? Disbelief? Maybe all three. *You wouldn't dare.*

"Oh, I would. Especially if you don't stop perving on my wife."

You're no fun. Ashton popped out of existence just as quickly as he'd popped in. Only this time instead of making Atlas grateful for the visit, he was annoyed. His brother had crossed all of Atlas's lines.

"Care to explain?" Payton asked. "Am I correct in assuming you saw a ghost?"

"Yeah, but not just any ghost. It was my brother. He's excited about the pizza."

Payton and Alison exchanged looks, and the both of them turned to him at the same time and said, "You were going to banish him over pizza?"

"Yes," he said and left the room.

Atlas walked out the back door, welcoming the sting of the chilly temperatures. The blue skies had turned cloudy, and the clean scent in the air meant one thing—snow. Normally he would welcome the reprieve of an imminent storm. Snow days always helped him relax. The peaceful blanket of snow always calmed him and gave him a chance to slow down without any of the guilt that often crept in when he took time off.

But today, all he felt was trapped.

He'd known for months that his time with his grandmother was limited. It was why he'd spent as much time with her over the last year as he could while finishing a tour. And why he was here now. He'd seen her tired and exhausted plenty of times. But today, after she'd put that ornament on the tree, she'd seemed almost as if she was just going to disappear. Like her life would slip right through his fingers, and it had unnerved him.

Atlas had done his best to pretend as if everything was fine. It was easy to do when Payton was around. She was full of life and a kindness that just seemed to draw him in. Made him think, even if just for a moment, that it was not just okay, but necessary to enjoy the hell out of this weekend. To create and treasure this time with Gigi and his family.

But then his brother had shown up, and suddenly all he felt was defeated. Like he wasn't doing enough to help Gigi. Just like he hadn't been there to help his brother. All the therapy in the world hadn't taken away that feeling that if he'd just been in that car, if he'd just been with Ashton, maybe, just maybe, things would have turned out differently.

Or we'd both be dead.

Atlas turned and eyed his brother. "I hate it when you read my mind."

I don't read minds, remember? I can just tell what you're thinking by that look on your face. How long are you going to torture yourself?

"Forever," Atlas said honestly.

I don't know why you're out here brooding over something that happened over a decade ago. If I were you, I'd be in that kitchen, flirting with the pretty chef.

"Isn't that what you were doing already?" Atlas gave his brother an impatient look.

I've got to get my kicks where I can. He smirked at Atlas. *For what it's worth, I think what you're doing is a good thing. I saw how animated Gigi was. She's thrilled. What's the harm in letting her think you're settled?*

"What if she's like you and never actually leaves? She'll know it was a farce." It was something that had just occurred to Atlas, and he felt like a complete idiot.

That won't happen, Ashton said, sounding definitive.

"How do you know?"

Ask yourself, Alistair, in all these years since my accident, have you ever seen another ghost?

"No. But I did when I was a kid."

You don't see them because of me. Don't you realize that?

"I suspected as much, but surely Gigi is different. You wouldn't really keep me from seeing her, would you?"

I'm not intentionally keeping other spirits away from you now, Alistair. Ashton's brow furrowed. *I don't know exactly what it is, but I think because our energy is connected there isn't any room for other ghosts.*

"Oh." A wave of utter sadness washed over Atlas. He'd just assumed that when Gigi passed, that wouldn't be the last time he saw her. The urgency to make sure she had the best weekend, that he savored every last moment with her, consumed him.

I thought you should know, Ashton said, giving his brother a sad smile as he faded away again.

Atlas glanced back at the house and thought of how animated Gigi had been when she'd heard the news that he'd gotten married. Of how happy she seemed to be when she met Payton, and he had to admit that he wouldn't change a thing. Operation Fake Marriage was his highest priority for the weekend. He just hoped the gorgeous blonde in the kitchen didn't get cold feet.

He heard the door open and turned around, hoping it was Payton. When he spotted his sister, he wrinkled his nose and said, "Oh, it's just you."

Alison rolled her eyes as she came to stand next to him. "You okay?"

"Sure. Why wouldn't I be?"

"You seemed… a little irritated," she said mildly.

He blew out a long breath and forced himself to glance

at her. His sister was staring at him with a sympathy that he hated. "Don't look at me like that."

"Like what?" she asked.

"Like you're about to force a therapy session on me."

She chuckled softly. "Okay, maybe. But it's only because I'm worried about you."

"You don't need to worry. I'm fine. I always am."

Alison was silent for a long moment, and he knew she had something to say. She was just waiting for her opening.

The silence dragged on, and finally he couldn't take it anymore. "Just say it."

His sister took his hand and squeezed. "You're allowed to be happy, Atlas. You know that, right?"

"I'm happy," he said automatically. "What's not to be happy about?" He grimaced and, in a quiet voice, added, "Besides what's going on with Gigi, I mean. But I don't think that's what you were talking about."

"No, it isn't." She leaned into him and put her head on his shoulder. "More often than not, you get like this when Ashton shows up."

"Ashton was pushing my buttons," he said, intentionally misinterpreting what she was saying.

She snorted. "I know. He's good at it. But that's not why you're upset. It's because he always pops up more when you get close to someone. And no doubt that's happening now because of Payton. You know it's okay to send him away, right? To not let him interfere?"

A pang of guilt hit him right in the gut, and his insides started to churn. "I'm not going to tell my twin's spirit he's not welcome. You know I can't do that, Alison."

"What happened that night was *not* your fault, big brother. I know I've told you that before, but I'm going to keep telling you until it really sinks in."

Snowflakes started to flutter from the sky, and Atlas fixated on one, watching until it landed in the water and melted instantly. The words that he always held in finally slipped past the lump in his throat. "Part of me knows that. My head does. My heart doesn't. But that's not the issue." He glanced at his only remaining sibling. "You're not a twin, so I don't think you can understand this, but Ashton is a part of me. A part of my soul. Losing him was..." He shook his head. "Devastating doesn't cover it. It was like losing half of myself. But then he returned. Or at least his spirit did, and when he's around, I feel whole again. I can't just send him away. Whoever I'm with will just have to learn to live with him popping in whenever he wants."

"You mean Payton will have to learn to deal with it, right?"

He grimaced at his rookie mistake. And then because he didn't know how to cover, he made a crazy face at her with his tongue out like he'd done when he was eight.

Alison laughed. "You're such a child."

"Nothing wrong with that. It keeps me young and wrinkle-free."

She peered up at him and then ran her fingertips over his cheek and up to the corner of his eye. "Sorry, bro, but it looks like you've got crow's feet. Those faces are probably what gave them to you."

He threw his head back and laughed. Damn, he loved her. "You're great. You know that?"

"I do. Too bad you're a doofus," Alison said with a nod as she slipped her arm through his and held on tightly.

He snickered. "You had to ruin the tender moment, didn't you?"

She shrugged, and as they walked back toward the door, she added, "Payton really is lovely, you know."

"She is," he said, wishing he'd met her under different circumstances. There was just something about her that intrigued him. Something that made him comfortable in his own skin. Maybe after this was all over, he'd ask her out for real. He chuckled to himself at the absurdity of dating his pretend wife.

"What's so funny?"

"Nothing," he said, even as he mentally planned a trip to Hawaii when this charade was all over, where he'd have Payton McCabe all to himself.

CHAPTER 6

"*P*ayton, you didn't have to make everyone lunch," Patty said, but her eyes lit with delight as she took a seat at the table. "You really made this pizza just from the random ingredients in the kitchen?"

"I did. It was no big deal," Payton said shyly and then glanced at Atlas. She hadn't seen him since he'd disappeared after the ghost incident. Ghosts weren't necessarily a problem for her. There was one that lived at the inn, but she mostly just haunted Olivia. Still, Payton had seen her a time or two. They had an understanding. Payton would put out a cookie or two at night for her, and the ghost left the kitchen alone. It worked for Payton.

"Payton has the magic touch," Atlas said.

"Literally," she added with a smile. "I'm an earth witch, and the trick to cooking for me is to just add a little bit of magic to whatever I'm making. It comes out perfect every time."

"Oh, isn't that lovely." Atlas's aunt leaned over and clutched his hand. "You're a lucky bastard. I'd take extra care to not lose this one."

He blinked at her, looking slightly offended.

Payton chuckled then softened her expression, hoping she sounded sincere when she added, "No danger of that. He's stuck with me now."

Alison chuckled and gave Payton a wink.

Payton smiled at her, grateful for the support.

"Look who's here," Atlas's cousin Danny called from the living room.

"I was already here, Daniel," Gigi said, clutching his arm as they slowly made their way toward the table. "No one needs to be announced after they return from a short nap."

"My apologies, Gigi," Danny said, giving her a solum nod.

Gigi glanced at the table and then at Atlas. "Did you have this catered?"

"Nope." He reached over and squeezed Payton's hand. "My bride did this. I tried to order food, but she overruled me."

"I just love being in the kitchen," Payton said. "It was nothing."

"It looks like a lot more than nothing," Gigi said. Danny helped her take a seat at the head of the table. Once she was settled, she looked around and asked, "Can someone get me my afternoon coffee?"

"Sure." Payton had already pushed her chair back and gotten to her feet when Gigi stopped her.

"Anyone but Payton," Gigi said. "The chef doesn't serve. Not in this house."

"It's okay. It'll just take me a minute." Payton was so used to cooking and serving everyone she cared about that it was foreign for her not to.

"Danny," Gigi said. "Please get me a coffee. Payton, please take a seat. There's something I want to talk to you and Alistair about."

"Sure, Gigi." Danny gave Atlas and then Payton a pointed look before he headed into the kitchen.

Payton slowly lowered herself back into her chair, nerves suddenly taking over. What was that look from Danny about? Had Gigi found out the marriage was a fraud? If she had, Payton resigned herself to the fact that she and Atlas deserved every bit of wrath Gigi was going to rain down on them.

Gigi leaned forward, placing her elbows on the table as she clasped her hands together.

"What is it, Gigi?" Atlas asked, looking just as nervous as Payton felt.

Gigi's lips curved down into a slight frown as she met his gaze. "I know you're a grown man, Alistair, and you have a right to choose which moments of your life you want to share with your family. I would never begrudge you that. I know that keeping your private life private has been challenging these last few years. It makes sense that you and Payton would do whatever was needed to protect your big day."

Atlas chewed on his lower lip and gave her a slight nod.

"With that said, I don't think I need to tell you just how much it would mean to me and your sister to share this moment with you both," she continued.

"That's why we're here, Gigi," Atlas said carefully. "To celebrate and to enjoy the holiday."

"Good," she said, grinning. "I'm glad you see it that way, because we have a surprise for you." Danny placed her coffee in front of her and she glanced up, giving him a nod of appreciation. Once she had her coffee mug cradled in both hands, she beamed at Atlas. "While we're all here, we decided to put on a surprise wedding for you and Payton."

"What?" Payton blurted before Atlas had a chance to say anything.

"Don't worry, dear," Gigi said with a glint in her eye. "We've handled everything. All you have to do is relax and enjoy the festivities."

"And humor us by renewing your vows already," Alison added with a chuckle. "I can't wait to hear what kind of vows Atlas wrote. Did they have something about the moon and the stars in them?"

Payton was speechless as her gaze darted from Alison to Gigi and then back to Alison.

"They did, didn't they?" Alison said, throwing her head back and cackling. "He's so predictable."

Atlas cleared his throat. "Let me get this straight; you just want a small family gathering where Payton and I say our vows again?"

"Yes," Gigi said and took a sip of her coffee.

"I guess that's okay," Atlas offered, and Payton wanted to

hit him over the head with her cast-iron frying pan. "Right, Pay?"

Payton hated being put on the spot. She desperately wanted to decline. It was one thing to pretend to be his new wife. It was entirely another to reenact an event that never actually happened.

"I set it up for Sunday afternoon," Gigi said, turning to Payton. "We'll also need the names and numbers of the relatives you'd like to be here."

"My family?" Payton squeaked out.

"And if you have any friends you want to be here, just let us know. I'll take care of all of it." Alison beamed as if she'd just dropped the news that Payton was getting a pony for Christmas.

"Um, well, I..." She trailed off, not knowing what to say. Surely Atlas was going to shut this down, right? He wasn't really going to let them throw a wedding, was he?

Gigi laughed softly. "I know it's a lot to take in, Payton."

"You have a brother in town, right?" Alison said. "I can get in touch with him. All we need to know is if there is anyone else you want to invite."

"No. I mean, yes. Olivia, his partner," Payton said as she pressed her hand to her chest, trying to keep her heart from beating right out onto the table. "But let me tell them. I want to... uh..." She struggled to figure out what to say and then finally settled on, "Hear their voices when I tell them. I'm sure they'll be shocked." That was a massive understatement. "I don't have any other family, and I'm kind of new in this town, so..."

Atlas cleared his throat. "Maybe we shouldn't do that. I was really hoping to just spend the weekend celebrating the holidays together."

"We will celebrate, Alistair," Gigi said, looking tired again. "Please just do an old lady this one favor. I had given up hope that I'd get to see you waiting for your bride at the altar." She turned her head, glancing at the lake. "It would make a wonderful wedding, don't you think?"

"Yes, it would," Payton said, nodding. There was just something about the wistfulness she saw in Gigi's eyes that made her willing to go along with the plan. Even though panic was pooling in her gut, she didn't want to disappoint the sweet woman who'd welcomed her so warmly into her family. Besides, Declan and Olivia already knew this weekend was a sham. What harm could it do to indulge his grandmother this one last wish? She pasted on a pleased smile and reached out to cover Atlas's hand with her own. "I'm willing if Atlas is."

Atlas stared at her for a long moment. His face was expressionless until he finally looked at his grandmother, gave her a soft smile, and said, "Anything for you, Gigi. What do you need us to do?"

She pressed her frail hands together as her eyes glittered with happy tears. "Nothing. We're handling every last detail."

The doorbell chimed, and Alison said, "Talk about timing." She stood, smoothed her long blond hair, and hurried from the room.

Payton sat back in her chair, wondering what she'd just gotten herself into. Then she glanced at Gigi's empty plate and stood, hovering over the food. "Gigi," she said. "What can I get you for lunch? We have pizza or salad. Unless you just want to snack, then in that case we have a variety of salamis, cheeses, and olives."

"You're kind, dear. Just a little bit of salad. And a roll if you have any."

"I do." She busied herself getting the older woman some lunch.

Atlas stared at her the entire time, studying her as if he were trying to work out a puzzle. She gave him a confused glance and shook her head slightly as if to say, *stop analyzing me.*

"Payton?" Alison called.

Payton glanced up and spotted Atlas's sister in the doorway that led to the living room. Just behind her was another woman who wore black-rimmed glasses and had her black hair tied up in a neat bun. "Yeah?"

"This is Blake, the stylist we hired," Alison said. "She's going to help you find a wedding dress."

"A wedding dress?" Payton didn't know why it hadn't occurred to her that she'd need to wear something appropriate at the wedding ceremony. Probably because she was doing everything in her power to block that part out.

"Yes, silly. She brought a bunch of options. Come with us so you can try them on." She waved impatiently at Payton.

"Right." Payton first retrieved a roll from the basket she'd set on the table and delivered lunch to Gigi. Then she gave Atlas a pointed look. He shrugged and mouthed, *you agreed to this.*

Dammit. What had gotten into her this weekend?

The promise of a half-million dollars that was going to save her and Declan's restaurant. That's what. She straightened her shoulders, stuffed all her guilt away, and joined Atlas's sister for an afternoon of playing dress up.

CHAPTER 7

*P*ayton was perched on a chair in another bedroom that was just as nice as the primary suite she was sharing with Atlas. There was a large king-size bed at one end and a sitting area with a view of the forest at the other. But the best part was the giant walk-in closet. Or she thought it would be the best part if it wasn't holding over two dozen wedding dresses.

"Are you planning to wear your hair up or down?" Blake asked, already grabbing Payton's hair and twisting it up so that it sat on the top of her head.

"Uh, I hadn't really thought about it," Payton said and reached for her phone that had just started buzzing.

"How did you wear it on the big day?" she asked.

"Big day?" Payton parroted as she looked at the incoming text. It was from Olivia.

How's it going?

Payton grimaced and typed, *911. I'm trying on wedding dresses.*

WTAF is going on over there?

"The big day," Blake said, sounding impatient. "You know, the day you got married?"

"Right." Payton quickly typed back, informing her of the impromptu wedding ceremony. Then she put her phone down and gave the stylist her full attention. "Our wedding day was pretty spontaneous, so I didn't have time to get my hair done. I just wore it down and put some soft curls in it."

She nodded. "Okay, so what I'm hearing is that you don't have your heart set on a specific hairstyle."

Payton blinked at her, wondering who prioritized a hairstyle over a wedding dress.

Blake seemed to read her mind, and she chuckled. "You'd be surprised how particular some brides are."

"Oh, I'm aware. I only deal with the food and the occasional wedding cake, and that's as close as I care to be to any Bridezillas." Payton smiled at her as she started to relax.

"Do you cater weddings?" the stylist asked, looking excited. "I'm always looking for great people to recommend."

"No." Payton shook her head. "I'm head chef at The Enchanted, an inn here in Christmas Grove. Ever since Priscilla Cain and Leo West were married there last New Year's Eve, we've become sort of a hot spot for weddings. To be honest, it's been a little stressful juggling the kitchen and the catered weddings, but we're managing."

"You're the chef at The Enchanted?" Blake's eyes got

wide with excitement. "Your pies are delicious. Is there a way to place an order for the holidays?"

Payton beamed and pressed a hand to her heart. "You have no idea how wonderful it is to hear you love my pies. Thank you for that. Unfortunately, there's not a way to order them... yet. But I'm working on a plan. It's just going to take a bit of time to get it all worked out."

Blake pumped her eyebrows suggestively. "I'm sure that new husband of yours is keeping you busy."

Heat stung Payton's cheeks, and she looked away, not at all sure what she was supposed to say to that.

But Blake just laughed and disappeared into the walk-in closet. She poked her head out. "Payton, are you coming?"

"Sorry." Payton scrambled out of the chair and wondered when she was going to stop acting so awkwardly. Probably not until the weekend was over and she was back in her kitchen, making risotto and pies. She followed Blake into the closet and stopped in her tracks at the sea of white.

"I know it's overwhelming," Blake said. "But don't worry, I'm going to pull some selections based on which silhouette you like best. Sound good?"

"Sure?" Her answer came out more like a question.

Blake snickered. "You're gonna get through this."

"I hope so."

After flipping through a dozen dresses, Blake produced five different styles and asked which Payton liked best.

Payton wasn't sure how to answer that. Every one of the dresses appeared to be either drowning in tulle or overrun with beads and crystals. "I don't know, Blake. I'm not a huge

DEANNA CHASE

fan of the puffy, princess dresses. I'd probably go for something simpler if you have it."

"I do," she said with a nod as she studied Payton. "I know you just told me simpler is better, and I'll certainly give you dresses like that to try, but would you mind humoring me and just trying on one with a bit of fanfare? You are marrying a rock star, after all. You deserve to feel like a princess for a day."

Didn't most rock stars marry models? And didn't most of them wear the sexiest dress they could find? But she figured it would be better to be drowning in fabric than to be put into one that left nothing to the imagination. "Yeah, I'll try it on. What else do I have to do today?"

"Excellent. That's what I like to hear." Blake shooed her out of the closet, and when Payton entered the bedroom again, she nearly knocked Alison right off her feet.

"Oh, no! Alison, are you okay?" Payton asked, grabbing her arms to keep her from toppling over.

"Yeah," she forced out. "But I'm not sure the champagne is."

They both glanced at the pristine white carpet and the golden liquid that was pooling at Payton's feet.

It took Payton just a second to react, but when she did, she went right into service mode. She snatched the bottle, set it on one of the side-tables, and ran into the bathroom to get a damp towel. Five minutes later, the spot had vanished and the rug looked good as new.

"Wow. That was impressive. How'd you do that without leaving a stain?" Alison asked.

"Earth witch," Payton said. It was all the explanation that

56

was needed. While she couldn't manipulate the carpet, she could do something about the champagne.

"You're handy to have around."

"That's what Olivia says," Payton said with a chuckle. "I guess it's good to have job security."

Alison gave her a confused look. "Job security? Won't you be leaving once Atlas is back on the road?"

"That's not—"

"Are you ready to transform into a butterfly?" Blake asked, sweeping out of the closet with a giant dress that looked like it would swallow Payton whole.

Payton turned to her, relieved to have been saved from the conversation with Atlas's sister, and said, "Absolutely."

"Perfect." Blake nodded to a small platform riser she'd set up in front of three portable full-length mirrors. "Get out of those clothes, and then once we get you into the dress, stand on that, okay?"

Payton did as she was told and then tried not to grimace when Blake placed the dress on the floor for Payton to step into it. She did as she was told, but no matter how hard she tried, she found herself tripping over the yards of fabric that made up the skirt.

"Here," Blake said, moving some of it to make it easier. "Just step into the middle, and I'll do the rest."

"Easier said than done," Payton muttered, but eventually she made it into the center of the voluminous dress and then stood still while Blake wrestled her into it.

"Wow," Alison said, staring at Payton with unshed tears in her eyes. "You're just gorgeous."

Payton raised both eyebrows, wondering how Alison

was unable to notice that the dress had enough fabric to form a hot air balloon.

"Oh my, goddess, Payton." A familiar voice sounded from the doorway.

Payton glanced over and spotted Olivia standing there with her hands pressed to her cheeks. Her furrowed brow and the pity on her face told her everything she needed to know before she ever even looked in the mirrors. "Olivia? How did you know where the cabin was?"

"Declan," she said and strode over to her friend. "I told him about your text, and he tracked your phone and sent me right over. Sorry to be stalkerish, but..." Olivia glanced at the other two women in the room. "We both just wanted to give you moral support."

"Don't be sorry," Payton said, more relieved than she thought possible. "I'm glad you're here for this."

"Oh, is this your friend?" Blake asked as she side-eyed the tall, raven-haired woman.

Payton nearly laughed. Olivia was dressed in sweats and a tattered sweatshirt, the one she wore on the days she went to the new gym in town. Her hair was up in a ponytail, and she hadn't bothered to put on a stitch of makeup. "She's more like my sister-in-law."

Alison clapped her hands together. "This is perfect." She held her hand out to Olivia. "I'm also Payton's sister-in-law, so we should be fast friends."

Olivia shook her hand, and then once the formalities were over, she turned to hug Payton and whispered, "I hope this dress isn't your favorite, because I'm going to have to veto it. You look like a marshmallow."

Payton cackled and said, "No way in hell."

"Good." Olivia let her go and then stepped back and asked, "Where's the champagne?"

Alison pointed to the half-empty bottle on the end table.

Olivia grabbed a couple of glasses and then the bottle. As she lifted it, she eyed the contents and said, "Looks like I have some catching up to do."

Alison let out a forced chuckle. "We haven't actually had any yet. I spilled some."

"All the more reason to start drinking," Olivia said with a wink as she grabbed one more glass and started to pour.

An hour and a half later, Payton had endured more than enough of both the champagne and the wedding dresses. They were on the second bottle and had been through eleven dresses. Not one had been anything she'd described. Simple. Elegant. Sexy, but not too revealing.

And it looked like number twelve wasn't going to hit that mark either. Payton stepped up on the riser and stared stone-faced into the mirror.

"This one is an illusion dress," Blake said, sounding wary as she took a polaroid picture to add to the rest of the stack. She said it would help Payton decide if she could see pictures of herself in all the gowns. But all Blake had done was waste film, because Payton wasn't going to wear any of them. She'd sooner get married in jeans and a hoodie. Blake tugged and pulled and cinched Payton into the dress and said, "You're fully covered, but the nude fabric makes it look like your skin is showing through in strategic areas."

"I know what an illusion dress is," Payton muttered as she eyed the heavily beaded, curve-hugging dress that made it look like she was one wrong move from a wardrobe malfunction.

"You look hot in this," Blake said. "If you're trying to drive Atlas crazy, this is probably the one."

"Except there isn't anything simple or elegant about it. Not to mention modest," Olivia chimed in and took a long sip of her champagne.

Olivia was just as irritated at the stylist as Payton was.

"She's fully covered," Blake snapped. "It's as modest as one gets."

"Except for the fact that she's having a nip-slip right now," Alison said with a hiccup and then a giggle.

Payton glanced down and just shook her head when she spotted the problem. There was nude fabric that covered most of her body between the cutouts. However, the bodice was made only of sheer fabric, boning, and crystals. One wrong move and the crystal was no longer doing its job.

Payton just shook her head. "This definitely isn't the one. And honestly, if this is what you think is modest, then I think we're done here."

"But—"

Alison popped up out of her chair and strode over to the stylist, her back straight, and said, "Thank you, Blake. But none of these are going to work. We'll email you some ideas this afternoon, and you can come back tomorrow for another try."

"But I brought all the hottest dresses for this year," Blake said with an air of superiority. "That's what I was told to do. If you want me to come back, I'll have to charge extra."

Alison waved a hand, indicating it didn't matter. "Be

here at eight in the morning. We can't spend all afternoon on this. We have a packed schedule already."

Payton gave Alison a grateful look and reached out to squeeze her hand. Payton squeezed back and then went to help the stylist deal with all the dresses. Once Payton was back in her own clothes and Alison was busy walking Blake out, Payton collapsed into one of the chairs, feeling as if she'd just gone three rounds in a boxing match. As it turned out, Payton wasn't cut out for dealing with temperamental stylists who got their feelings hurt when the client had their own ideas of what they felt comfortable wearing.

Olivia moved to perch on the edge of the matching armchair and leaned toward Payton as she said, "Declan and I are worried."

"About what?" Payton asked and then sat straight up as worry washed through her. "The restaurant? Did something happen with Matisse?"

"No, it's not the restaurant," Olivia said, waving her hands as if trying to clear the air. "The deadline is still the end of the month. Nothing's changed. We're worried about you and this wedding."

Payton glanced away. "It's a *fake* wedding, Olivia. It'll be fine."

"But this is a lot more than you signed up for. No one said anything about a wedding. You shouldn't have to walk down the aisle for the first time to a man you don't love. That's just... We both want you to know that you don't have to do this. Not for the restaurant. We'll figure something else out."

"We both know there's no other option to come up with

the money before the end of the month," Payton told her friend.

"You don't know that. We could maybe find another investor. Zach Frost or even Holly Reineer and her husband. The people of Christmas Grove want Apollo's to succeed."

Payton couldn't even imagine asking Zach Frost to invest. He'd just heard she'd married one of the richest men in the music industry, and his cousin to boot. Wouldn't that be a fun conversation as to why her husband wasn't supporting her?

"No," Payton heard herself saying as she shook her head. "I don't want anyone else tied to the restaurant. My worst nightmare is that this would happen again. Or the partner would start trying to interfere with how we want to run things. I want, no I *need*, this restaurant to be a success, Olivia. I want to stay here in Christmas Grove. Grow old here and raise a family. All of that takes putting down roots, and that's what we did with the restaurant. I'm not ready to risk it just because I don't want to wear a marshmallow wedding dress."

"We both know it's not the wedding dress that's the problem," Olivia said softly. "It's that this has gotten out of hand, don't you think? And neither Declan nor I want you to feel forced to do something you don't want to do."

"You know what's funny?" Payton asked her, suddenly feeling lighter about the entire situation.

"That you had a major nip-slip while wearing a burlesque dancer's wedding dress and the stylist called it modest?"

Payton snorted and then laughed even harder.

Olivia chimed in, and by the time they recovered, they both had tears staining their cheeks.

"Damn, Olivia. That was brutally accurate." Payton snickered once more and then sobered. "I was going to say that what's funny is that while I am doing this to save the restaurant, that's not why I agreed to the fake wedding. It was because of Gigi, Atlas's grandmother. She just looked so... happy. And I didn't want to take that away from her. Not now. Not in her final days. I suppose I'm even willing to dress up like a marshmallow if I have to."

"Goddess no!" Olivia cried. "That's where I draw the line. I get that you have a heart of gold and that's why you're doing this, though I still think it's a little insane. But my opinion is irrelevant. You've made up your mind, and Declan and I will support you. On one condition."

"What's that?" Payton asked, feeling her anxious nerves start to settle.

"You have to promise you won't wear a dress that looks like a marshmallow, a cupcake, or a chandelier, no matter how often that stylist tells you they're all the rage. Hold out for one you won't feel like an alien in."

"Okay. You got it. Anything else?"

"Yes, one more thing," she said, her face dead serious.

"Well?" Payton dug her nails into her thigh as she waited for Olivia to spit it out.

"When the officiant says, 'you can now kiss the bride,' I demand that you kiss the hell out of that man, because if you don't, I will."

"You're going to kiss Atlas Mazer if I don't?"

"Someone's got to," she said, fanning herself. "That man is sex on a stick."

Payton sat there stunned for just a moment before she said, "Olivia, I love you, but if you come near my fake husband, I'll poison your morning coffee."

Olivia laughed. "Okay then. Message received. Now make sure you give him something he can't forget. Got it?"

"Got it." Payton gave her a mock salute and then held out her hand to her. "Come on. I'll show you how to get out of this house of horrors so you can report back to Declan. Tell him he needs to be here to give me away Sunday afternoon."

"He'll love that," Olivia said dryly.

"It won't be the first time I've given him heartburn," Payton said. "Make it up to him, would you?"

They were both still laughing as they left the temporary bridal shop and headed outside.

ou look sharp. Ashton was lounging on the bed, propped up against the headboard with his feet crossed at the ankle.

Atlas let out a derisive snort. "If you say so."

No one would believe the rock star Atlas Mazer was wearing a suit. You almost look respectable.

"Let it go, Ashton," he said, not wanting to have this conversation. There was a reason why Atlas embraced the rock star wardrobe of ripped jeans and tight T-shirts.

Ashton rose from the bed and walked over to the windows, staring out at the lake. *I like her. When this contract is up, you should date her for real.*

"My life isn't conducive to dating. You know that. It's not fair to leave someone behind while I go out on the road for months at a time." Atlas said the words he'd said a dozen or more times in his life, but there wasn't much conviction behind them now. The truth was he did want to date Payton. He just didn't know how to make it work.

Aren't you tired of one-night stands? I know you, Alistair. You need connection.

"I connect to the fans." Atlas walked over to the mirror to check out the suit one last time. It would do. He quickly changed into his signature jeans and a graphic T-shirt and then went to stand next to his brother. "I know you didn't come here to counsel me about my love-life."

Ashton chuckled. *Who else is going to tell you to get your head out of your ass besides me?*

"Alison is happy to do that for you. Now tell me why you're really here. Do I need to get my notebook out?" Atlas already knew the answer and didn't bother waiting for Ashton to respond. He just walked over to the bed and picked up the notebook that was sitting on the nightstand. "What's the theme today?"

Darkness.

A sharp stab of pain hit Atlas right in the chest. He pressed his hand to his heart, trying to soothe the ache, but he should have known from experience that the gesture was useless. Darkness was a theme Ashton had explored over and over in his songwriting. In fact, Atlas's biggest hit to date was a song called "Cloaked in Midnight." It was about the veil between life and death.

I follow you down the rain-slicked cobblestones, Ashton said as he paced the room. It was always how he worked.

Atlas wrote down the lyric and waited. He knew better than to inject his ideas when Ashton was working out a song. It would only agitate his twin, causing him to flame out. If that happened, it could be weeks before Atlas saw him again. And as much as he wanted his life all to himself sometimes, he wanted his twin nearby more.

The midnight rain cuts me to the bone.

The shadows of you...

Have forever served as my only muse.

Atlas stifled a tired sigh. It had been years, and every song that poured out of Ashton was about Chloe, his high school sweetheart. The one he'd left behind to pursue his dream of being a rockstar with Atlas. Every major hit Atlas ever had was a song about Ashton's girlfriend. The one neither of them had seen since the day they'd driven off to southern California to cut their first album. But she was in the words that Atlas sang night after night for nearly a decade.

The desire to walk out and go find Payton hit him hard. He didn't want to do this again. The very idea of putting out another song about Chloe was enough to make him want to quit music altogether. But he couldn't walk out on his brother. He owed him this. To be his vessel, so that Ashton's art could live the life he couldn't.

We're young, forever young.

Suspended in time...

Forever a prisoner in their minds.

Young, we're destined to be forever young.

By the time Ashton was done voicing his lyrics, Atlas was already working out the guitar arrangement in his head. And although he still didn't love the idea of working on this song, he walked to the closet and pulled out the acoustic guitar that was never far from his side.

Ashton continued to pace the room while Atlas plucked out a haunting melody to match the vibe of his lyrics. Just as Atlas started the chorus, Ashton said, *Add a drawn-out drumbeat there.*

Atlas nodded and made a notation in his songbook.

After fiddling with it for over an hour, Atlas finally played the entire song. When he strummed the last notes, Ashton nodded. *Yes. That's it.*

"What's it called?" Atlas asked, knowing the title would be nonnegotiable. They never were on the songs that Ashton wrote.

Skipping on Cobblestones, he said and then vanished into the ether.

"Brilliant," Atlas said to himself. The juxtaposition of the haunting song with the childlike title would create the kind of buzz that money couldn't buy. His brother was a musical genius. There was no doubt about it.

Atlas always wondered what would have happened if Ashton hadn't died just as his career was getting started. Would he be the one who was an international superstar? Probably. It was all of his songs that had propelled Atlas and his band into the stratosphere. Sure, some of the songs Atlas had written were hits, but not like Ashton's.

But then again, if he hadn't died so suddenly at such a young age, would his brother have ever written such haunting songs? Atlas had no idea. All he knew was that his life's trajectory had been forever changed that night. He'd lost his twin, his best friend, his other half, and it had devastated him. He'd been ready to give up music for good after that, but then Ashton's spirit had shown up, pulled him out of his grief haze, and demanded that he get on his feet and have the career that they'd both dreamed about.

Atlas sat in one of the chairs and absently started to strum on the guitar. It was an upbeat melody this time. One that made him tap his feet and gave him a sense of joy. Those types of songs were a rarity for him, but absolutely necessary to keep him going.

Summer drenched days.

I ran wild, lost in a young man's haze.

You said love like there's no tomorrow.

Give your heart with wild abandon.

Never fear sorrow.

You've got to risk something to gain what's platinum.

Don't wait to fill your promises of tomorrows.

Atlas put the guitar down, and just as he grabbed his notebook to record the bridge he'd been working on, he heard someone start to slow clap. He jumped up out of the chair and spotted Payton standing in the doorway.

"What are you doing there?" he asked, sounding harsh even to his own ears.

"Sorry!" She held her hands up in a defensive gesture. "I didn't mean to spy on you. I was coming in to grab a sweater and was transfixed listening to you. Were you working on a new song?"

Dammit. He hadn't meant to bite her head off. "No apology necessary. I'm the one who should be sorry. You startled me is all. I don't usually work on songs in front of an audience. I like to have the song pretty much ready to go before I play it for anyone."

"I shouldn't have intruded," she said as she strode across

the room and into the closet. She appeared a few seconds later, wearing a bulky sweater.

He raised both eyebrows. "Are you going somewhere?"

"No. Why?"

He scanned her body before he met her eyes again. "You look like you're bundling up for the cold."

"Oh, right." She wrapped her arms around herself and rubbed lightly. "No, not going anywhere, but I did walk my sister-in-law out a few minutes ago, and since then I haven't been able to shake off the chill."

"Your sister-in-law was here?" That was news to him. Had anyone else crashed the surprise wedding weekend? Anxiety flared to life, making Atlas's fingers twitch. The more people who were clued in on his lie, the more chance it had of leaking. He didn't so much care about the public. Not for himself anyway. He just didn't want to disappoint his grandmother.

"Yeah, Olivia came to save me from the great wedding dress disaster," she said with a humorless chuckle. "Without her, I'd either look like a marshmallow or I'd be a walking wardrobe malfunction."

"That sounds precarious," he said, amused. "The hunt for a wedding dress couldn't have been that terrible, could it?"

Payton gave him an involuntary shudder. "You have no idea. We sent the stylist out to find some more options. If she doesn't succeed, I'm going to wear jeans and fuzzy boots. Hope you're okay with that."

"Only if I get to wear my ripped jeans and a clean T-shirt," he shot back instantly with a grin.

Payton walked over to him and gave him a high-five. "I'd

give anything to just wear jeans to this thing, but something tells me your grandmother wants us to play up the fantasy with the tux and white dress."

"No tux," he said, absently reaching for the tie that wasn't there around his neck. "They talked me into a suit though."

She raised her eyebrows at him this time. "Got something against tuxes?"

"Yeah," he said with a laugh. "The last time I wore one, I ended up in the tabloids for months with them all claiming one of the groomsmen ran away with the bride. It ruined tuxes for me."

Payton's eyebrows shot up "*Did* you run away with the bride?"

"Sort of." He gave her a sheepish smile. "But only because she was running anyway and needed a ride. I took her up to Washington State and dropped her off with the guy she described as 'the one that got away.' Then I left and went back into the studio."

"You took her to Washington State? From where?"

"Los Angeles. It was a long drive, but it was fun. I heard she ended up marrying that guy. They have two kids now. So I guess it was my good deed of the year."

"Not for the guy who got left at the altar," Payton said, making a cringy face.

"Definitely not. He was the band's accountant, and because of all the drama, he ended up in the papers. It turned out he was wanted for embezzlement in another state, so Peg dodged a bullet and so did the band. When we looked over the books, we learned he hadn't taken anything yet, but the plans had been laid out, and if he'd worked for us any longer, we'd have been screwed. In the end I was labeled a hero. But all those tux pictures were trauma inducing," he said with a laugh.

"I can see why," she said, shaking her head. "Well, at least you've got a suit picked out. I'll give you a heads-up if I have to resort to jeans, then at least we can match."

"I'm down. Shake on it?" He held his hand out to her, completely charmed. In fact, he was more relaxed than he had been all day, and it was all because of her. She'd gotten him talking, and honestly, that was rare for him. Payton didn't treat him like a rock star. She hadn't ever been starstruck either. He liked that she talked to him like he was a normal person and not someone to either worship or take down a notch for reasons they could never articulate.

"Absolutely. We'll go down on the jean-clad ship together." She shook his hand, and he couldn't help but hold it a beat or two longer than necessary.

Payton looked down at their connection and then back up into his face. "Your fingers are callused. That's kind of hot."

Atlas's lips curved into a slow, appreciative smile. "You think so?"

"Yes. Definitely."

He brushed his thumb over the top of her thumb and said, "Let me know if you're interested in the full body experience. I'd be happy to show you just exactly how hot my callused fingers can be."

Payton threw her head back and laughed. Tears actually shown in her eyes as she tried and failed to get ahold of herself. Finally, she sucked in a breath and forced out, "Do you really think that was sexy?"

He couldn't help grinning at her. "You didn't think so?"

She wiped at her eyes. "No. Not in the least."

Atlas nodded thoughtfully. "In that case, I look forward to proving you wrong."

CHAPTER 9

"*T*here you are," Alison said as she barged into the bedroom where Payton and Atlas were still chuckling at his attempt to flirt with her.

Payton just couldn't get over the complete lack of game from the rock star. Though she supposed he was so accustomed to having women throw themselves at him that he was probably severely out of practice.

Atlas glanced at his sister and gave her a suspicious look. "What exactly do you people have in store for us now? Is there a vow writing workshop we're supposed to attend or something?"

"Vow writing?" Payton asked, feeling a light sweat break out on her forehead. They had said something about vows earlier now that she thought about it. Only she didn't have any, and the idea of coming up with something had her head swimming.

"Stop freaking your bride out," Alison told her brother.

DEANNA CHASE

Then she turned to Payton. "He's just being a smartass. We all assumed you'd just say whatever you said when you got hitched the first time."

"Yeah, sure," Payton said, wishing she was doing anything other than pretending to marry a man she hardly knew this weekend.

"Don't sound so excited," Alison said with a smirk. "If your vows were X-rated, I'm sure you'll find many other wonderful things to say about this doofus. If not, let me know. We'll ask Gigi to come up with some nice things to say about him."

"You're going to ask my grandmother what my wife should say about me?" Atlas asked, sounding scandalized. "Isn't that a little... I don't know, weird?"

"Why?" Alison smirked at him. "She's the only one who likes you enough to have good things to say about you."

"That's just rude, Alison," Atlas said with a sniff then turned to Payton. "Don't ask Gigi. If you need inspiration, go online and check out my fan boards on Reddit. You'll find more than enough inspiration."

"More like fan fic," Alison said under her breath and then winked at Payton. "Don't listen to us. I'm sure you've uncovered plenty of loveable things about my stinky brother. I mean, after all, you did marry him. He must have some decent attributes I haven't been made aware of."

"Yeah, it's called great sex, Alison," he said dryly.

Payton choked on her own spit. "Okay. That's enough of that. I'll be just fine, thank you both."

The pair of them cackled like nine-year-olds.

She shook her head at them but couldn't help laughing

along with them. She too had a brother, and she recognized their good-natured teasing.

"You're lucky you haven't scared her off," Atlas told his sister as he gave Payton a half-grin.

"I suppose it's all that great sex," Payton deadpanned. "I know women who have dated way worse when life-changing orgasms were involved."

"Oh no!" Alison plugged her ears with both fingers and shook her head violently. "You did not just say that about my brother. Take it back."

Payton stood there with both hands in her front pockets. "Can't. It's already out there."

Atlas glanced down at his crotch and added, "Well, not yet, but if my sister would take the hint and leave, then maybe."

Alison's whole body shuddered before she cried, "Enough! You got me. I won't ever say anything again about your manly prowess."

"Prowess?" Payton echoed, enjoying Alison's discomfort far more than she should.

"You know what I mean." She shook her head. "That's enough of this conversation. I actually came back here for a reason other than to be harassed."

"Harassed? You started this," Atlas said.

"Whatever. Just come with me. Both of you. And bring your winter gear. We have a surprise for you."

"Winter gear?" Payton asked, almost afraid to find out what they had in store for her next. "That sounds an awful lot like ice skates or snow skis. I don't do either, so if that's what this is, then—"

Alison held up her hand, cutting Payton off. "It's not anything athletic. I promise. Just wear whatever will keep you warm while you're outside."

Atlas glanced at Payton and gave her an apologetic look. "If you need a hat or gloves, let me know. I'll let you use mine."

"I'm good," Payton said as she went to the closet to retrieve her long red coat. When she stepped inside, she was hit with a flashback of the sea of white wedding dresses she'd been subjected to earlier in the afternoon. Her blood pressure rose, and she could feel her pulse ticking beneath her skin. If the stylist once again tried to make her look like an over-decorated cupcake the next day, Payton was going to have to let Atlas know their jeans pact was on in full force.

Shaking off the memory, she found her coat, and after patting her pockets to make sure her knitted cap and her gloves were there, she retreated to find Atlas alrcady drcsscd in a long black wool coat and a green scarf. He wasn't wearing a hat, but he was holding a pair of gloves.

"You look hot," she said, meaning it. The coat made him look sophisticated, but his wild dark hair still afforded him his signature rock star style.

"Hot?" He cocked one eyebrow. "Payton McCabe, are you hitting on me?"

"Maybe just a little bit." She slipped her arm through his and added, "Let's go find out what the surprise is. If it's something awful like ice fishing, let's just make a break for it. Deal?"

"Ice fishing?" Atlas shook his head. "You do realize that the lake isn't frozen, don't you?"

"Yes, but with witches around, you can never assume anything."

"That's true. Okay, you have a deal. If it's ice fishing or anything else equally as horrifying, we'll hightail it out of here and hit the town. How's that sound?"

"Perfect."

They strode down the hallway arm in arm until Atlas stopped at one of the rooms. He knocked softly and said, "Gigi?"

"Come in, Alistair," she said so faintly that Payton barely heard her.

Atlas opened the door and took a step in. Payton followed and spotted his grandmother already in bed with the covers tucked tightly around her. She had the remote in her hand and a cup of herbal tea on the nightstand.

"I just wanted to check on you and see how you're doing," Atlas said. "Find out if you need anything."

"No, honey. I don't need anything other than Bruce Willis on my TV for my annual holiday screening of *Die Hard* and for you and your bride to go have a lovely night."

"Oh, a *Die Hard* Christmas movie truther," Payton said. "I knew I liked you."

Gigi gave her a bright smile. "It's how I like to start the holidays. It reminds me of my late husband."

Payton moved without even thinking. She paused at the side of the bed and held out her hand to Gigi. The older woman seemed to be moving slower, but she managed to grab Payton's hand and squeeze. Payton squeezed back and said, "I'm sure your husband is here and more than pleased with your movie pick."

Gigi glanced at Atlas, hope shining in her watery blue eyes. She wanted to know if Atlas could see her late husband.

He gave her a slight frown and shook his head. "Not that I'm aware of, Gigi. But you know that I haven't seen any spirits other than Ashton since the accident."

"Oh, that's right. I must've forgotten." Gigi pointed the remote at the television and hit the power button. "Come here and kiss my cheek," she ordered Atlas.

He did as he was told, wished her a good night, and then left with Payton trailing behind him.

"This way!" Alison said cheerfully. She opened the back door and waved them both out into the cold.

A light dusting of snow was falling from the sky, and a large blue moon peeked out from behind the gathering storm clouds.

"Okay, we're out here. Now what?" Atlas asked her.

"Just wait for it." She clasped her hands like a giddy teenager.

Payton glanced around, wondering where the surprise was, and when she didn't see anything, she asked, "Okay, what are we expecting? Is a herd of reindeer coming to put on a show? Because that would be impressive."

"Especially if they were named things like Rudolph, Comet, and Vixen," Atlas said.

"Now that would have been a great idea," Alison said. "I'll put it on the list in case we need another wow factor."

"Need?" Payton asked. "You don't need to wow me about

—" Payton forgot she was even speaking when she spotted the horseless sleigh that had flowers covering every single inch of it. "Oh. Em. Gee. Wow!" she said, overwhelmed by the thoughtful gesture. If this had been a *real* impromptu wedding, then Payton was sure it would've been an event that she'd never forget.

The sleigh stopped right in front of her. Atlas jumped up in it and held out his hand to her. "Can I help you aboard, Ms. McCabe?"

She smiled up at him, amused by his sudden British accent, and said, "Yes, please. I'd be delighted."

Atlas helped her in with ease. As soon as she was seated, the horseless sleigh took off at a slow pace, giving her time to take in all the lights bouncing off the lake. And the two puffins who looked so serene, floating off in the distance.

Payton felt like she was in a dream. And when she spotted the singing and dancing snowmen, she knew she was in for the time of her life.

CHAPTER 10

"*I* can't believe they did this," Payton said, her eyes alight with wonder.

Atlas gazed out at the snow-covered terrain and the enchanted snowmen dancing to "Santa Baby" and shook his head in disbelief. "It's a little over the top."

"I think it's amazing." Payton leaned her shoulder into his and bumped him lightly. "Don't be such a stick-in-the-mud. It's fun."

"It is?" he asked in a teasing tone. "Do you want to dance with Frosty?"

"Can't."

"Why not?"

She looked him up and down, smirked, and said, "Because Mr. Frostypants is sitting here in the sleigh and I have a strong suspicion that if we danced right here, we'd end up toppling over, right into the snow."

"You really think a rock star can't dance?" he asked,

completely charmed by the woman sitting next to him. There wasn't anything better than a woman who wasn't afraid to speak her mind. "Is that a challenge, Payton McCabe?"

She eyed him, her eyes twinkling in the moonlight. "I'm not going to believe you can twirl like those snowmen unless you prove it."

"Stop the sleigh," Atlas said.

The sleigh slowed to a stop as the snowmen continued their dancing. Atlas hopped down and held out a hand to Payton. "May I have this dance, Ms. McCabe?"

A smile claimed her lips as she reached for his hand. "I'd be delighted, Mr. Mazer."

The sound of Atlas's stage name sounded wrong on Payton's lips, and he found himself volunteering his given name for the first time in years. "It's Frost, actually."

"What?" She stared up at him in confusion.

"My last name." He reached up and tucked a lock of her hair behind her ear. "My legal last name is Frost. Not Mazer. I thought my wife should know that."

Recognition dawned in her eyes as she chuckled. "Right. I remember reading that in the marriage contract." She winked at him. "I guess Mr. Frostypants really is a fitting name. I'm going to be using it for the rest of the weekend."

"Not if you expect me to answer." He slipped his arm around her waist, grabbed her hand, and then started to glide her around the clearing.

She let out a small gasp of surprise as Atlas literally swept her off her feet. Her cries of delight filled him up inside, and Atlas wanted to stay in that magical moment forever. When her feet finally touched the snow-covered ground, Atlas spun her around a few more times before letting her come to a stop right in front of him.

Payton's hands came to rest on his chest as she gazed up at him, her eyes locked on his.

"Was that proof enough?" he asked, his voice low and full of sex. The voice he used on stage to seduce the crowd.

"Are you trying to seduce me, Mr. Frost?" Payton ran her hand up to his neck and then trailed her fingers over his jaw.

"Frost? Not Frostypants?" he asked, pulling her in closer.

"Oh, there's nothing frosty about you right now, Atlas. And you know it."

His lips curved up into a slow smile as he leaned in, stopping just an inch from her lips and then pausing.

Her breath hitched, and he knew he had her.

But still, he whispered, "Do you want me to kiss you, Payton?"

She let out an irritated huff and then buried her hand in his hair, pulling him in the last inch.

Atlas took her mouth and immediately got lost in her. She was sweet and demanding and molded against him. Every inch of his body was alive with desire for her.

The kiss was heated, full of passion and something else he couldn't quite put his finger on. Something new and different that he'd never felt before. Something that just made him feel... right.

When he finally pulled away, they both stared at each other, a mix of shock and awe passing between them.

"Well," Payton breathed. "That was..."

"Incredible," he finished for her.

Her lips curved up into a ghost of a smile. "I was going to say hot, but incredible is good, too."

He chuckled, and when movement caught his eye, he glanced past her at the snowmen. They were still dancing, but their movements had changed. They were now paired up and— "Payton, look." He turned her around so she could witness what he was seeing.

"What the—oh my gods, are they doing what I think they're doing?"

"I think so."

She pressed a hand to her mouth as she laughed. "They're mimicking our dance. Look, that one is sweeping the other off its feet."

Atlas pointed to the right. "Those two look like they're going to melt their faces off."

Payton giggled when she saw the two snowpeople getting a little X-rated as they kissed. "They do look like they're enjoying themselves."

"That one over there is getting a little frisky," Atlas pointed out as one of the snowmen reached around and squeezed what could possibly be the rump of the other one.

"Okay, now that definitely didn't happen when you kissed me," she said, turning to look at him again as she shook her head. "These snowpeople have a mind of their own."

"*I kissed you?*" Atlas challenged. "I seem to recall that you were the one to instigate that situation."

She raised an eyebrow and gave him an incredulous

look. "We both know you started that. I was just the one to finish it."

"That you did." He nodded to the sleigh. "Are you ready to see what else they have in store for us?"

"I am."

Once they were back in the sleigh and it started to roll again, Payton turned to him and said, "Thank you for the dance. It was lovely."

"You're welcome." He draped his arm along the back of the seat and eyed her. "That'll teach you to question a rock star's moves."

Payton snorted. "You did not just say that."

He just grinned at her.

"You're a cocky bastard, You know that, right?"

"Sure. But you like it."

Payton rolled her eyes, but he didn't miss the way her lips were curved into a small smile or the flush that colored her cheeks.

They were silent as the sleigh moved alongside the lake, taking in all the cabins that were decorated with Christmas lights. When the wind picked up a little and Payton shivered, Atlas checked under the seat and came up with a blanket. He gestured for her to move in closer to him and then draped it over both of them. "Better?" he asked.

"Yes." She pulled the blanket up higher and curled into him.

Enjoying the moment more than he knew he should, he wrapped his arm around her shoulders and trailed his fingers up and down her arm.

"So, Alistair Frost, tell me, how did you get into music?"

she asked, looking up at him with curiosity. "School? Church? Or were you just naturally drawn to it?"

Alistair Frost. That was an identity he'd tried to leave behind many years ago. After he'd lost Ashton, he just hadn't felt like he'd been that person anymore. Half of him was gone. It was why he'd chosen a stage name. Why he'd chosen to become someone else. Usually, if anyone other than his grandmother or Ashton called him that, he recoiled. Withdrew back into himself, back to the days after he'd lost his brother. It was always unnerving. But this time, hearing his name from Payton's lips, all he felt was *seen*.

It was both unnerving and deeply comforting.

"Atlas?" she asked, sounding concerned.

"No, call me Alistair," he said, looking down at her. "I like hearing you call me by my real name."

Her features softened as her lips curved up and her eyes crinkled at the edges. Looking pleased, she said, "All right, Alistair, are you going to tell me how you got into music? Were you a prodigy, or did you work day and night to hone your guitar skills?"

"Prodigy?" he chuckled. "Hardly. Actually, it was my brother who started up with the drums. He begged for years for a drum kit, and when we were thirteen, my mom finally caved and set him up in the garage. It only took two weeks of him banging away on them for him to decide we needed to form a band. But my mom didn't have money for any more instruments, so Ashton found an old acoustic guitar at a garage sale and demanded I be his guitarist."

"And how did you feel about that?" she asked.

He shrugged, remembering the day he and Ashton

YouTubed how to restring the guitar and fumbled around with it for hours. "I was game. I mean, what thirteen-year-old doesn't want to be in a rock band?"

"But Ashton was the driving force?"

"Definitely. He was already writing songs and had us on a practice schedule." He chuckled softly. "He was so committed to that damned schedule. Imagine being fifteen and your brother throwing a fit when you end practice early because you have a date with the girl you've been crushing on for over a year."

"Any chance he was throwing a fit over the girl and not practice?" she asked.

"Nope. None. Ashton was singularly focused on music. It's all he ever wanted, really. Sure, he dated, but the girls in his life always came second to his art. There were some days when I wanted to strangle him."

"Sounds like a true artist then," she said and then hesitated before adding, "From an outside perspective, it looks like maybe you've adopted that same mentality."

"You think so?" he asked, frowning at her.

"Have you ever had a long-term relationship?" There was no accusation or judgment in her tone, just genuine curiosity.

"No, but that's mostly because I'm just so busy. It's hard to date with my schedule and commitments."

"Commitments you readily agree to," she said gently.

"Yeah, but…" He trailed off, realizing she was right. Atlas never turned down opportunities and had been on the go for well over a decade. But he was so successful that he knew he had enough leverage that if he wanted to slow down, his label wouldn't stop him. They'd be disappointed, but they'd go along with whatever he wanted just to keep him on the roster. They wouldn't take the risk that he and the band would sign with another label.

"It sounds to me like the music gig wasn't just your brother's dream." She shifted away from him and gazed out at the magical night. "Look," she whispered. "Reindeer."

Atlas glanced over to where she pointed, and sure enough, there was a herd of reindeer standing near the shoreline of the lake. They were watching the sleigh curiously as Atlas and Payton slid on by.

"It's really not," Atlas said. "My dream, I mean."

Payton narrowed her eyes and studied him with fascination. "Music wasn't your dream?"

He slowly shook his head. "No, not exactly. It was Ashton's dream, and when we were younger, I was happy to go along with it all. But I was mostly in it for him."

"And now?"

He glanced away, watching as the nearby trees lit up with white twinkle lights. How did he answer that question? Walking away wasn't something he'd ever considered. How could he when Ashton was still writing songs? "Music is my life."

"Sure," Payton agreed. "But do you want it to be?"

"It *has* to be," he said, meeting her gaze. "As long as Ashton keeps writing songs, I'll keep singing them."

CHAPTER 11

*P*ayton stared at Atlas, her mind racing. "Are you saying that all your songs, even the current ones, are written by Ashton?"

"No, not all of them, but a lot of them are." He strummed his fingers on his leg as he added, "He wrote one today while you were trying on dresses."

"He did?"

Atlas nodded. "He wrote the lyrics, and I worked out the musical arrangement. That's usually the way it happens." He blew out a long breath. "There's a reason why I still put his name on all the song writing credits. His portion goes to various charities."

"Wow, that's..."

"A little crazy that I write most of my songs with a ghost?"

"No," she said quickly. "Not crazy at all. I was going to say pretty special."

"It is," he agreed, staring at his strumming fingers again.

Payton reached over and pressed her palm to his cheek, gently turning his face so that he was looking at her. "And probably really, really hard for you."

"Yeah," he said with a scoff. "It's really rough being a rock star. Who'd turn that down?"

"A lot of people," she said quietly. "The question is, if it weren't for your brother, would you?"

He started to shake his head, but then stopped. He grimaced. "Dammit, I really don't know. The truth is I haven't given it much thought. Ever since Ashton died, I've just carried on, fulfilling the dream. Living life for the both of us. It's what I do."

"That's honest at least," she said with a soft smile. "Maybe someday you'll take a breather and really ask yourself what *you* want, Atlas. Everyone deserves their shot at happiness."

"I'm happy," he said, sounding defensive.

She wasn't so sure about that, but she didn't push it. Who was she to tell him how he should navigate his life? Besides, being an internationally loved, highly successful musician was hardly a hardship. "Okay."

"Okay? What does that mean?"

Yeah. He was definitely defensive. "It doesn't mean anything other than okay. You said you're happy, and I'm taking you at face value." She chuckled softly. "I mean, why wouldn't you be happy? You're on a romantic sleigh ride with your lovely wife, enjoying dancing snowpeople, twinkle lights, and actual reindeer. It's pretty magical, right?"

His entire body seemed to relax and the tick in his jaw

disappeared. "It is pretty magical. I have to give you that."
He glanced up and laughed. "Look."

Payton tilted her head back and let out a small gasp of
surprise. "Seriously? Shooting stars?"

"It appears that my family thought of everything for this
sleigh ride," he said. "Now make a wish or two."

There was only one thing on Payton's mind when she
wished upon one of the shooting stars. All she wanted was
enough money to save Apollo's, her and Declan's restaurant.
She silently put that wish out into the universe, praying her
wish was heard.

"Did you make your wishes?" he asked.

"Yes, but I just have one wish. I don't need anything else."
As soon as she said one wish, a faint voice in her head said,
and Atlas Mazer. Her pulse quickened and suddenly her skin
felt hot, despite the chilly night air.

"Just one wish?" he asked, raising both eyebrows. "Surely
there's something else you want in this life. Love? Fame?
Fortune?"

"I don't need fame or fortune," she said.

He looked at her thoughtfully. "So, love then. You should
wish for it."

"What about you? Did you wish for love?"

"Nah." He turned to stare out at the darkened forest. "I'm
too busy for love."

"At the moment, so am I," she said truthfully. "Maybe
when things slow down."

"Life never slows down, Payton," he said, still not
looking at her.

"It will. Eventually."

"I have my doubts." There was a finality to his tone.

Honestly, so did she. But as he pulled her in to snuggle against his chest, she realized that life *had* slowed down. That in that very moment, all they had to do was sit in the sleigh and enjoy both the magic of the season and each other. It was those moments that made the rest of it worth living.

"Tell me about your dreams, Payton. What do you really want?"

Payton didn't know why, but she was surprised by his question. No one ever seemed to care enough to ask her what she wanted out of life. And to have the larger-than-life rock star be the one who was asking was more than a little surreal. "That's easy. I want to put roots down in a small town, where everyone knows everyone else, and become part of the fabric of the community."

"You crave stability?" he asked.

"Yes," she said with a nod. "My parents were... volatile. While we were growing up, I don't think Declan or I ever felt like we had solid footing. We just never knew what kind of household we'd be walking into at the end of the day. Would our parents be fighting? Loved up and acting like no one else existed? Or completely ignoring each other and us as well? It was always a tossup. And because they were known for causing scenes, we were the talk of the town for several years. After my father left, I thought things would get better, but things were very unstable financially, and life was just stressful all the time."

"And that's why you want to live in a small town?" Atlas asked and shook his head. "It seems after all that you'd want

94

to run as far and as fast as possible to the nearest city, where everyone wasn't always in your business."

Payton laughed. "You know, that's exactly what Declan did for years. He didn't want anything to do with any small town, and certainly not Christmas Grove. After I broke my leg, I had to beg him to stay for a while to help out. He definitely didn't want to, but in the end, he did it for me."

"And in the process found the love of his life in a small town and stayed?" He wrinkled his nose. "That sounds an awful lot like every other Christmas movie out there."

"It does, doesn't it?" she said dreamily. "Who doesn't want to star in their own Christmas movie love story?

"Me." He raised his hand, making a face that implied he was horrified.

She laughed. "I hate to tell you this, rock star, but you're already doing that this weekend." Payton waved a hand around at the snowpeople who were back again. Half were waltzing about while the other half were still imitating Payton and Atlas.

"I guess it's not so bad." He winked at her.

She cast a glance at two of the snow people who were busy kissing and then smirked at him. "Probably better than not so bad, but I'll take it for now."

"You're probably right. Who would have thought we'd get to witness a snowpeople make-out session. This is going to be a night to remember."

"You know what, Alistair Frost?"

"What's that, Payton McCabe?" he asked, his eyes glinting.

"I think I like hanging out with you." Payton hadn't

expected to feel so at ease with Atlas, but here she was, flirting and telling him stuff that she never talked about with anyone. Maybe it was the magical sleigh ride. Or the late hour. She wasn't sure, but all she knew was that she didn't want it to end.

"You're not so bad yourself."

A light snow started to fall, and a snowflake got caught in his eyelash. Without thinking, she reached up to gently brush it away. But when she did, his lips gently brushed over her palm, causing goosebumps and sending a shiver of desire over her skin. She paused, watching him.

He held her gaze and pressed one more kiss to her palm before pulling away and clearing his throat. "Sorry. I probably shouldn't have done that."

"Just like you shouldn't have kissed me earlier?" she asked, disappointed that he was backtracking from his attraction. Though she knew it was a terrible idea to get romantically involved with her fake husband, she couldn't help wanting him. Atlas Mazer was not the man she'd thought he was when she'd met him way back on New Year's Eve. That man had been a cocky and entitled, albeit charming, celebrity.

This man, the one sharing the sleigh ride with her, was deeper than she imagined and very attentive. The fact that he'd asked about her dreams and was so interested in what she had to say was more than a little surprising. She'd met her share of celebrities, and while some had turned out to be truly wonderful people, the ones who had Atlas's level of fame usually were so out of touch she hadn't been able to relate to them at all.

But Atlas? She admired his deep connection to his twin and understood his deep desire to be there to help Ashton achieve his dreams even in his death.

"It's true, I probably shouldn't have kissed you," he admitted and then twisted his lips into a cocky grin. "But I wouldn't change it even if I could."

"Good," she said. "Neither would I."

His gaze dropped to her lips, and Payton couldn't help but dart her tongue out to moisten them.

Atlas groaned and quickly glanced away. "Don't do that."

"You started it," she said.

"I know, but now I'm trying to behave."

"That's disappointing," she teased.

"It is, isn't it?" he agreed. But then he narrowed his eyes at her, and in that oh-so-sexy husky voice of his, he said, "When this weekend is over, I'm definitely taking you on a real date."

"After? Do you plan on sticking around Christmas Grove?" The fact was she knew she wouldn't turn down a date with the gorgeous man sitting next to her. But she would manage her expectations. He'd already told her that he was too busy for a relationship, and now that she knew his reasons for working as hard as he did, she understood why. There was no reason to believe that he'd be interested in settling down anywhere, much less Christmas Grove.

But she could have a good time while it lasted, right?

Sure, Payton, she thought. *Because you're so good at casual dating.*

This time it would be different. She knew what to expect. A fun weekend, maybe dinner and ice skating in the town square. Or even better, they could spend the day on a winter hike in the foothills. She liked getting him away from everyone else. When he was just Alistair Frost and not Atlas Mazer, the transformation was remarkable. She liked both personas, but Alistair Frost, the real man underneath the rock star façade was the one she found most interesting.

"I don't need to go back out on tour until after the new year," he said. "I was scheduled to play a couple of holiday gigs, but I canceled them. I want to be around if Gigi needs me."

"So you are leaving... when?" She blinked at him. "Sunday? After the wedding? Won't she be suspicious when I'm not there?"

He shook his head. "No, she knows you're a chef and have a job to do. The only thing that will bother her is that she'll try to shoo me away to go spend time with you, but I'll refuse."

"And she'll be secretly glad that you do," Payton added.

"Definitely," he said with a nod.

"Where does she live?"

"Arizona. But she grew up in the California foothills. It was her idea to come up here for the weekend. She's missed it."

"Arizona for Christmas, huh?" She tried to imagine what it would be like to decorate cactus with twinkle lights and couldn't help the chuckle that escaped her lips.

"What's so funny?"

"Nothing, I just... It can't feel like Christmas in Arizona when she grew up with this." Payton waved a hand at the magic laid out in front of them. "It's not Christmas without snow, hot chocolate, and warm gingerbread cookies."

The sleigh came to a sudden stop as the snow flurries fell harder all around them, even as they remained completely dry and snowflake free in the sleigh.

"What's hap—" she started. But then there was a flash of light, and suddenly they were both holding hot chocolate and a tray appeared in front of them with an assortment of not only gingerbread cookies, but sugar cookies and shortbread too. "Oh, this is incredible."

He nodded. "Yes, it is. And so are you."

Her face flushed. "Stop flirting with me, Atlas. You're going to make me really like you. And then in just a few short days, you and your sweet grandmother will be leaving. My heart can't take it."

"Is that so?" he asked, looking amused again as he took a sip of the hot chocolate.

"Yes, it is. You're going to put some sort of holiday spell on me, and then when you leave, I'll be ruined for anyone else who might actually ask me out in this town."

His flirty expression vanished, and he suddenly looked bothered.

"What? Was it what I said about being ruined? Because I was just kidding. You know that, right? I'm—"

He silenced her with a possessive kiss. His free hand cupped the back of her head as he pushed his chocolate flavored tongue past her lips.

Payton was powerless to do anything other than meet his demands. Now *this* was a kiss. He was making her his with just his tongue, and she was more than willing to submit. Every inch of her was alive and wanted him.

When he pulled back, he pressed his forehead to hers and whispered, "I think I forgot to tell you something."

"What's that?" she asked, breathless.

"When my family leaves to go back to their lives, my grandmother and I are planning to stay here in Christmas Grove."

"You are?" Her brain was scrambled, and she wasn't sure she was processing information the way she should.

"We are. So do me a favor?"

"What's that?"

He ran his thumb gently over her cheek and said, "Don't accept any dates unless they're with me."

"Oh," she said, finally catching on. "You don't want your grandmother to find out we aren't actually married. I get it. Sure, no problem. I haven't had a date in... Gosh, I don't know how long. It's—"

Atlas pressed his fingers to her lips, silencing her. "No, Payton. It's not because of that. We'll be here, not out in town where she'd see you with someone else."

"Then why?" she asked, confused.

He chuckled softly. "Isn't it obvious?"

"Well, not really."

"Because, Payton, I really like you, and if anyone takes you out, I want it to be me. Not for show. Not to convince my grandmother. But because I like you and want to see you again. Is that okay?"

She grinned up at him. "Yes. I'd love that."

"Even though you know I'll be leaving soon?" he asked, and his brow furrowed with worry lines.

Payton touched her fingers to his lips, just as he'd done to her moments before, and said, "Don't worry, Atlas. I'm well aware that the rock star has commitments he has to uphold. But I'd very much enjoy the chance to spend more time with you and share everything I love about Christmas Grove."

"Good," he said. "I think I'd like that too."

"And don't worry," she added quickly. "I'm not going to fall for you. I promise."

He sucked in a breath and let it out slowly. "That's really too bad. I think I would've liked that, too."

CHAPTER 12

"Are those... elves?" Payton asked, peering over the edge of the sleigh.

Atlas squinted at what he thought was a small animal. But when it reached up and touched the wooden fence that separated the property from the neighbor, the fence was suddenly magically covered in a massive number of lights. The creature ran from the fence to a small spruce tree. With one zap of magic, gorgeous red and gold ornaments appeared on the branches along with perfectly tied red bows. A second zap of magic lit the lights, and a third produced an angel that started to sing "Silent Night."

Other voices chimed in, and suddenly the entire property was fully decorated, complete with a choir of angels atop the trees, filling the night with music.

"Wow," Payton whispered, leaning into him. "Your family made this happen?"

"Probably my Aunt Peggy. She's good at these things. Though the elves are a surprise."

"There are gnomes, too," she said, pointing to the back porch, where they were singing and swaying along to the music.

As soon as the song ended, the sleigh came to a stop. The elves disappeared and the gnomes turned to stone. The cabin had been trimmed in lights and all of the trees were glinting with holiday cheer.

"It's truly magical," Payton said as she stood.

Atlas jumped down and then grabbed Payton by the waist, lifting her down to the ground.

She let out a little yelp of surprise but then laughed as she stumbled into him.

His arms went around her, and his entire body warmed with pleasure when she pressed into him. That feeling of rightness swept over him again, and then out of nowhere, lyrics started to form in his head. It was rare that a song would just pour out of him, but as he gazed out at the lake with the snow falling softly around them, he started to sing.

"Under a blanket of December stars,
You were there, soothing my edges.
We came together, building our bridges.
It was a magical Christmas.
A night I just know I'll always remember."

HE HUMMED a few bars and repeated the words.

When the notes died away, Payton looked up at him. "It's beautiful. That's a new song, isn't it?"

He nodded. "It is."

"I hope you finish it. It's one I'd like to put on my playlist."

"What else do you have on this playlist?" he asked, curious to know if she listened to his other music. He never cared if other people in his life were fans of his music, but suddenly it was really important to him that she liked his art.

"You're fishing," she said with a chuckle.

"Maybe."

"Okay, I'll give you one. Want to guess?"

"It's one of my songs?" he asked, wanting to make sure they were on the same page.

She *tsked*. "Isn't that what we're talking about? You want to know if I'm a fan."

Ouch. She'd called him out on his egotistical BS. Not that he didn't deserve it. "One guess, right?"

"Yep," she said, nodding. "Which song of yours do you think I have on my playlist?"

"Hmmm." Atlas studied her as if her appearance might give him some sort of clue as to which song was her favorite.

"What are you looking at?" she asked with a small laugh. "Do you think I have it written on my forehead or something?"

"You do." He ran a finger just above her brow-line. "It says your favorite Atlas Mazer song is 'My Last Heartbeat.'"

Payton laughed as she shook her head and took a step back. "Nope. Not even close. Though Olivia really likes that one. It's a little too dark for me."

"Really?" Before, he'd just wanted to know if she was a fan. Now he desperately wanted to know which song was her favorite. "My Last Heartbeat" was one of the most successful songs in his catalog. It was also one that Ashton wrote. She was right; it *was* dark. All of Ashton's songs held at least a tinge of darkness. But if she liked lighter songs, ones that were more upbeat and held threads of happiness, then maybe there was a chance he wrote it. "Are you going to tell me which one it is?"

She pursed her lips and gave him a half shrug. "Are you sure you really want to know?"

"Oh, I want to know."

"Okay then—"

A bright flash of light illuminated the darkened night. Atlas quickly glanced around, wondering what magical surprise his family had concocted this time.

Payton clutched Atlas's arm and said, "Atlas, you have a visitor."

He glanced down at her and then followed her wide-eyed gaze and spotted his brother standing near the lake and holding up a glass of champagne.

"Ashton?"

His brother lifted the champagne glass, acknowledging him.

He turned his attention to Payton. She wore a shocked expression, but she kept her eyes locked on Ashton as her fingernails started to dig into his skin.

"It's all right," he soothed. "I know he's a spirit, but he's not going to harm you or anyone else."

"Harm?" Ashton asked, looking taken aback. "Nah,

brother. I'm just here to toast to you and your bride. It's about time you found someone who can put up with your selfish ass."

Atlas's good mood deflated instantly. Why did his brother have to show up at the end up what Atlas considered the perfect date?

"He's not selfish," Payton said, coming to Atlas's defense. "If anything, I think he's more generous than anyone I know. But thank you for the congratulations. We appreciate it."

Payton wrapped her arm around Atlas's waist, making it look like she was claiming him. And Atlas was surprised by just how much he wished that was true.

Ashton snapped his fingers, and two nearly full glasses of champagne floated right in front of them. Payton was the first one to reach up and grab one of the flutes.

Atlas followed her lead, and as soon as they both held the glasses up, Ashton said, "To the happy couple. May your marriage be one of love, trust, and laughter. He took a long sip and then faded into the night.

Payton downed her champagne and said, "Does that happen often?"

"You mean champagne appearing out of nowhere?" he asked.

"No." She waved at where Ashton had been. "Does he appear like that often?"

"Only once or twice a day," Atlas said.

"That's... a lot. It explains a lot."

"It does?" Atlas asked.

"Yeah, but it's not important." She set her glass down in the snow.

"You're right. It's not," Atlas said, happy to be off the topic of his brother. He didn't want to think about him in that moment. While he appreciated the toast, he didn't care for being interrupted. Nor did he want to think about why Ashton had appeared to Payton. As far as Atlas knew, Ashton never appeared to anyone except him. He'd find out later. Right now, all he wanted to do was focus on Payton. "If I recall correctly, you were just about to tell me which one of my songs is your favorite."

"I was?" she asked coyly.

"Yes. You wouldn't want to go back on a promise, would you?"

"I don't recall promising anything, Atlas Mazer," she said, her eyes glinting in the moonlight.

"So you're just going to torture me instead?"

She laughed. "I think if I tell you, *that's* going to torture you. Especially since it looks like we're sharing a bed tonight."

He envisioned the large bed in their shared room and nearly groaned. But then the implication of what she'd just said hit him and he stared at her, his skin suddenly hot. "Your favorite song of mine is 'Sex'?"

Her slow smile told him everything he needed to know. "Payton, are you trying to kill me?"

"You're the one who asked." She winked at him and then strode into the quiet cabin.

CHAPTER 13

*P*ayton heard Atlas's steps behind her as she hurried through the quiet house toward their shared bedroom. Her heart was hammering against her ribcage, and her mind kept echoing with that one word. *Sex. Sex. Sex.*

Why had she told him that "Sex" was her favorite song? Why had she been flirting with him so outrageously when she knew they had to share a room and a bed. As if she wasn't having enough trouble keeping her hands and lips off him. Now she wanted to jump him.

If she did, would he turn her down? She doubted it. The rock star had quite the reputation when it came to short-lived flings. And given that the attraction between them was palpable, it wasn't hard to imagine what would happen once they were alone.

No, she admonished herself. Atlas Mazer was paying her to act a part. Not to become his bed partner for the weekend. Payton wasn't going to allow herself to be reduced to some sort of high-class call girl.

When she finally reached their room, she hurried through and came to a sudden stop when she spotted the champagne bucket and the tray of chocolate-covered strawberries near the two armchairs that looked out over the lake. The lights suddenly dimmed as "The Way You Look Tonight" by Frank Sinatra started to play.

"That's a little over the top," Atlas said softly from behind her. "Isn't that something they usually save for the honeymoon?"

"How would I know? I've never been married." Payton walked over to the champagne, popped the cork as if she were an expert, and poured two glasses.

Atlas watched her, and when she gestured for him to join her, he slowly made his way to her side, seeming hesitant.

She held out one of the glasses.

He eyed it and said, "I'm not sure that's a good idea."

Payton raised both eyebrows. "Why? Do you have somewhere to be?"

"No. That's the problem."

"Oh, are you afraid I'm going to take advantage of you once you've had a drink or two?" she teased.

He snorted out a laugh. "Is that your plan?"

"Does that sound like something I'd do?" She eyed him as she placed her glass on a side table. Smiling to herself, she walked over to the bed and grabbed the thick fleece throw. After spreading it out in front of the floor-to-ceiling windows, she retrieved the chocolate-covered strawberries, grabbed her champagne glass, and then took a seat. "Care to join me?"

"A bedroom picnic? Are you serious right now?" he asked, amusement dancing in his eyes.

"Why not? Someone went through all the trouble to make these amazing chocolate-covered strawberries. Do you know how hard it is to get good strawberries in December? I'm not wasting them. And champagne and strawberries are my favorite combination, so..." She waved a hand, inviting him to take a seat. "I can't think of anything better than sharing this with a friend."

Payton held her breath, waiting to see what Atlas was going to do. She knew she was crossing the line from friends to something else by setting up the bedroom picnic. But she couldn't help herself. She'd had such a lovely evening with him, and she didn't want it to end.

Nor did she want to think about what would happen once they went to bed.

"You're asking for trouble," Atlas said as he took a seat on the throw next to her.

Beaming, Payton offered him a strawberry.

"Thanks." He took a big bite, closed his eyes as he savored it, and let out a tiny moan of pleasure.

Payton bit down on her bottom lip, never imagining that she'd be jealous of a damned strawberry. She tipped her champagne flute and downed the rest of its contents.

Atlas chuckled and leaned back on his elbows, staring out the window at the holiday lights illuminating the property.

"If you weren't a musician, what do you think you'd be

doing?" she asked, lying on her side and propping her head up with one hand.

He turned to her, a thoughtful expression on his face. "You mean if I'd gone to college and got a degree in something respectable?"

"Uh, no. That's not at all what I meant," she said, shaking her head and letting out a small chuckle. "I respect the hell out of what you do now. I just wondered where you think you'd be if music hadn't been it for you? Did you have any other dreams? Something you want to try, but haven't had time?"

He blinked, seeming surprised by the question. Then his turquoise eyes lit up as he turned to face her, giving her his full attention. "You know what? No one has ever asked me that question before."

"Not even Ashton?" Payton didn't get the impression that Atlas was close with many people. But his twin had been his person. She couldn't imagine that had changed in death.

"Especially not Ashton," he said, his tone somber. "There was never anything other than music for him. And since that's what he wanted to do, that's what we did." He shrugged slightly. "It hasn't been a hardship."

Payton blew out a breath and then gave him a wry smile. "I guess it worked out for you."

"You could say that." He winked. "But back to that question of yours. What would I be doing if I wasn't the front man of a rock band? You know, there is one thing I've always thought was really cool."

"Oh, yeah? What is it? Acting? Modeling? Politician?

Anywhere that puts you in front of a microphone or camera?"

"Seriously?" He smirked. "Is that your impression of me?"

"Kinda. You do command attention when you walk into a room. I assumed you'd want to be doing something where you're the center of attention."

"Do I sense a bit of judgment there?" he asked, clearly enjoying himself.

"No!"

He raised one eyebrow.

"Okay, maybe a tiny bit, but only if you wanted to be a model. If that was your goal, I'll just assume you wanted an excuse to show off those abs of yours on a regular basis."

"Damn, Payton. Bust my balls, why don't you." He was still laughing when he reached over and brushed a lock of hair out of her eyes. "I suppose I do let my stage persona take over when I'm trying to charm someone, but no, I have never wanted to act, model, or do anything at all in the political field. If I were going to choose to do something else, it would be to create something with my hands."

"What do you mean? Something like pottery?" she asked, surprised this was where the conversation was heading.

"Glassblowing," he said with a definitive nod. "There was a glassblowing shop next to this venue Ashton and I used to play all the time in the early days, and I always found it super fascinating. The idea that someone can shape something so beautiful out of molten glass is mind-blowing."

"Glassblowing," she said, both surprised and impressed.

"You do know there's a glassblowing shop in Christmas Grove, right? They do blow-your-own-ornament sessions. We could check them out while you're in town if you want."

"I want," he said, his expression deadly serious. "I'd go right now if you hadn't gotten me drunk on champagne."

Payton rolled her eyes. "Please, you haven't even finished one glass. So don't use that as an excuse when you hit on me later."

"Oh, we've reached the flirting stage of the evening," he said, eyeing her suggestively.

"No we haven't. Eat another strawberry," she ordered even as her face heated. Why was it she just couldn't help flirting with the man?

He opened his mouth and waited.

"Dammit. I walked right into that one," she said, willing herself not to touch the berries.

But when he glanced at them and then back to her with that smolder in his gaze, she caved and grabbed one. He opened his mouth again and waited.

"You think this is funny, don't you?" she asked as she held the berry out to him.

He made a show of taking the chocolate-covered fruit, chewing slowly, and moaning his appreciation.

"Okay, stop that, or we're gonna end up in some serious trouble," she said, gesturing between the two of them. "We need to keep this professional."

"You started this," he said.

"Well, now I'm finishing it." She hoped so, anyway. He was right. She was the one who couldn't seem to stop flirting.

"All right. How about you tell me one thing *you'd* like to do besides be a chef?" he said, surprising her.

She hadn't expected him to act interested in her life. Though why not, she couldn't say. He hadn't been anything but kind and attentive to her since they'd arrived at the cabin. She cleared her throat. "Does being a baker count?"

"You're saying that if you weren't a chef, you'd want to be a baker?" He rolled onto his back, clutched his middle, and laughed as if that was the funniest thing he'd ever heard.

Payton couldn't help it. She started to laugh, too.

When Atlas finally stopped laughing, he rolled onto his side and said, "What would you bake?"

"Pies. Lots of them." She didn't know why she was embarrassed, but her cheeks were hot and she was having trouble looking at him. "I want to open a pie shop."

His laughter faded away as he studied her. "You said you *want* to open a shop. That's different than what you'd do if you weren't a chef."

"That's true." She gave him a sheepish smile. "As much as I love running the restaurant at the inn, I'm finding the thing that gives me the most joy is when I can make people happy. My pies do that for people. Their eyes light up when they talk about them, and when people tell me they want to order them, they are usually telling me about some family event. It just makes me happy. The idea that something I create is part of a lasting memory… I don't know. It just fills my soul."

"I get that. It's not all that different from when someone finds meaning in one of my songs," he said. "There's joy in being the one to help people form connections. It's what's important in life."

Payton nodded slowly, feeling a sense of rightness wash over her. This moment, with this man, she just knew she was right where she was supposed to be. "Thank you. That was what I needed to hear."

"So, are you going to do it? Open that pie shop?" he asked.

"I'm going to try. Just as soon as we deal with this restaurant business, then I'll start thinking about the logistics."

He frowned. "What restaurant business?"

Oops. She hadn't meant to talk about Apollo's. She didn't want anyone in Christmas Grove to know that the restaurant was in trouble. It was her goal to get that loan paid off before there was any mention of bankruptcy. In the restaurant world, even a hint of trouble could start an avalanche. The restaurant had just opened and was doing well. Any rumors of trouble could cause a snowball effect. But Atlas wasn't exactly going to go around town telling everyone the restaurant might have to close. He was off in the cabin, pretending to be married to please his grandmother.

"Are you talking about your brother's restaurant?" Atlas asked.

She swallowed the lump in the back of her throat. "Yeah, only we own it together. It's nothing, really. Well, not nothing, but it will be as soon as we pay off a loan."

"And that's why you said yes to all of this?" he asked, already making the connection.

"Yeah." She let out a sigh. "It turns out our investor is going bankrupt. And if we don't buy him out, then our restaurant will be included in his assets, and there's a strong chance it would be put into receivership."

"Ouch."

"That's putting it mildly," she said. "But I'm here now, and hopefully by this time next week, we won't have to worry about that anymore. I can start making plans to build my pie empire."

He poured more champagne for both of them and then raised his flute. "To pies and taking over the world."

Grinning, she touched her glass to his and added, "To following dreams."

They held each other's gazes as they each took a sip.

Payton put her glass down and said, "There's no way I would've agreed to be your fake wife if there'd been another way to save the restaurant."

The light seemed to fade from Atlas's striking eyes. "I figured you had your reasons. In fact, I was shocked you actually agreed. You don't seem like the type of person who would agree to such a scheme under normal circumstances."

"You're right about that," she said, fingering the flute. "But I'm sure you wouldn't have had any problem filling the role. A rock star like you must have thousands of women who would do anything to spend time with you."

He let out a derisive grunt. "Sure. If I want to hang out with obsessive fame chasers. There's a reason I asked you, Payton, and not any of the people who stalk me online. I wanted someone real."

"Someone who your grandmother would believe you'd actually marry," she said, filling in the blank.

"Sure, but more importantly, someone I could actually hang out with. You were so unimpressed with me that night we met, I think I fell a little in love with you right then and there."

She rolled her eyes, knowing he was just charming her again. "That's enough flattery, Atlas. I'm already here. No need to keep laying on the BS."

He grinned. "See? Always calling me out. I like that."

She liked it too, and that was the problem.

They spent the next few minutes in comfortable silence, watching the lights twinkle outside. It wasn't long before Payton yawned and her eyes watered. It had been one hell of a day. Had he really just picked her up that morning from her house? Since then, she'd learned she was getting married on Sunday, met his entire family, decorated a tree, tried on wedding dresses, and had the best date of her life. It almost made her scared to think about what was in store for her the following day.

Atlas climbed to his feet, wincing as he pressed his hand to his lower back.

"Are you okay?" she asked, her brow furrowed in concern. "Did you hurt yourself?"

"No. It's just normal aches and pains from the years of touring. Back and knee pain is just part of the job, I guess. I'll be all right." He held out his hand to help her up. "You can take the bed. I'll make up a nest on the floor or something."

Payton looked up into his kind face and shook her head.

"No way. Look at you. You can't even stand completely upright after sitting on the floor for less than an hour. What will you look like in the morning if you sleep down there? You take the bed. I'll either curl up in the chair or make that nest you were talking about."

"No way." He shook his head and pressed his lips into a thin line. "Forget it. I will not have my wife sleeping on the floor."

"If you keep saying that, you're going to forget it's a lie," she said with a laugh.

"You might be right," he agreed. "But you're still not sleeping on the floor. How about we just share the bed? We're both adults. We can make a pillow wall, and I promise to stay on my side." He held up three fingers. "Scout's honor."

"Pillow wall, huh?" she asked thoughtfully. "Okay, fine. We can share. Just don't snore, or I might smother you in your sleep."

"No promises." He gestured for her to use the bathroom first and then got busy cleaning up their bedroom picnic.

Fifteen minutes later, Payton was lying in the bed, fully covered in her holiday cotton pajamas when Atlas emerged from the bathroom, wearing only his boxer briefs. She sucked in a sharp breath, and when he grinned at her, she turned away, embarrassed by her reaction. What exactly had she expected him to wear?

Pajama bottoms, maybe? But that wouldn't change anything. She'd still have been subjected to his well-defined chest, and her fingers would still be tingling to touch him.

"Don't worry, I'm used to it," he said as he slid into the bed.

"Cocky bastard," she muttered and turned away from him to face the windows.

He chuckled softly and then turned out the light.

Payton lay there a long time, listening to his soft, even breathing and resenting that he'd fallen asleep so easily. Meanwhile, all she could think about was the fact that he was just a foot away with only a pillow between them. She fidgeted and tossed and turned until she finally just got out of bed and moved to curl up in one of the chairs.

Her mind was racing with the events of the day, how comfortable she felt with Atlas, and how she wanted to burn the memory of their date in her mind forever. She was unsettled, feeling as if something important had just happened, something that was fleeting. And no matter how much she wanted to hold on to it, she worried it was destined to slip through her fingers.

Payton felt rather than heard Atlas move from the bed to where she sat in the armchair.

Without a word, he placed his hands on her shoulders and gently began to massage the tension away. His touch was everything she never knew she needed, and almost immediately, her eyes began to drift closed. Sleep had started to claim her, and just as she was about to slip under, Atlas tugged her up and led her back to the bed.

This time when they climbed under the covers, the pillow wall was gone and Atlas moved to spoon her from behind. He slid his hand down her arm until his fingers entwined with hers.

Payton knew she should move away from him, give herself some space from the man. But every inch of her body relaxed for what felt like the first time in months. Feeling warm and content, she closed her eyes and let sleep claim her.

CHAPTER 14

"Good morning, lovebirds!" Alison's annoying voice pierced through Atlas's thick fog of sleep haze. The woman beside him shifted in his arms as if she were trying to move away. Atlas tightened his hold, not ready to let go.

"Atlas," Payton said quietly.

He opened his eyes and looked at her, smiling at her sleep-tousled hair and the pillow line on her cheek. Damn, he loved the intimacy of waking up next to someone. Especially *this* someone. "Good morning." His voice was filled with gravel.

Payton glanced at the door. "Your sister is here, and you're just in your underwear."

He scanned his body, taking in the fact that he must've kicked the covers off at some point. "So? She's the one who barged in here." He smiled into her eyes and couldn't stop himself when he leaned in and gave her a soft kiss on the corner of her mouth.

Her eyes widened but she didn't pull away, and Atlas decided to take it as a win.

"Payton has to try on dresses in forty-five minutes, and Gigi is waiting to talk to you, Atlas," Alison said. "Get some clothes on, will you?"

The door closed with a soft click.

"Hi," Atlas said, tucking a lock of Payton's hair behind her ear. "Did you sleep okay?"

Her cheeks flushed, and a smile lit her sleepy eyes. "Once we came back to bed, yeah, I did."

"Good. So did I. Best night of sleep I've had in ages, actually." Not just ages. The truth was, he thought that was the best night of sleep he'd ever had.

"Me, too."

In the morning light, with no makeup on, Payton was so lovely that Atlas couldn't look away. The way her hair was cascading over her shoulder made him want to brush it back to give him access to start exploring every inch of her golden-kissed skin. Unable to stop himself, he reached up and ran his knuckles down her neck.

She closed her eyes as a small tremor ran through her body.

Intense satisfaction filled him all the way to his soul. Payton was just as affected by him as he was by her. "Sounds like we both have a busy morning."

She let out a sigh and rolled over onto her back, staring at the ceiling. "You have no idea how taxing it is to try to find a wedding dress. Especially when they all either swallow me whole or are destined for a wardrobe malfunction."

He let out a bark of laughter. "Wardrobe malfunction? Are we talking nip-slip or a flash of your snatch?"

Laughter ripped through her as she snorted her amusement. "I'm afraid that I tried on dresses that had the potential for either or both." She sat up and kicked the covers off to expose her legs. "See this right here?" She pointed to where her hip and thigh met. "There was a dress that was cut this high on one side. I kid you not. When I walked, everything, and I do mean *everything*, was on display."

"Can't say I'd be disappointed to see that," he teased.

"While I'm walking down the aisle with your grandmother watching?" she asked with one eyebrow raised.

"Maybe not with Gigi watching," he conceded. "But the wedding night? Hell, yes."

"I think I'd find something better to wear on the wedding night." She jumped out of the bed, and Atlas couldn't help but be disappointed as he watched her disappear into the bathroom.

There was no denying that he wanted her. If he had a choice, he'd keep her in the bed for the next couple of hours, exploring every inch of her body. But he couldn't. That wasn't why they were there at the cabin.

A bolt of guilt struck him right in the gut. What was he doing lusting after Payton? He was here in Christmas Grove to spend time with Gigi during her last days. To give her one last gift before she left his world. He muttered a curse, frustrated with himself as he climbed out of bed and headed for the closet.

Five minutes later, he was dressed, the bed was made, and he was sitting in one of the chairs, waiting for Payton to reemerge.

"Hey," she said, sounding surprised when she walked back into the bedroom. "Do you always make the bed?"

"No." He walked over to her, unable to keep his distance. Now that he knew what it was like to have her in his arms all night, he wanted more, much more. But as much as he craved her, he kept his hands to himself. Now was not the time. "Almost never, but that's because I'm usually hopping from hotel to hotel," he said, amused.

"So you do when you're at home? Or were you just trying to impress me?"

"Both," he said honestly, reaching out to smooth her hair. "I know you think I'm a spoiled rock star, but underneath all the hype, I'm just a regular guy who makes his bed every morning and cleans his own bathrooms."

She stopped mid-step and stared at him in disbelief. "Are you really trying to tell me you don't have housekeepers?"

He chuckled. "Okay, fine. I do have a service that comes in every two weeks, but that's mostly because I'm rarely there. Someone needs to keep the place up."

"Sure, whatever you say." She walked over to him, pressed her hand to his chest and said, "Tell your grandmother I said good morning and that I'll see you both for lunch."

He placed his hand over hers and leaned in, kissing her on the cheek. "Good luck finding a wedding dress that both covers your snatch and doesn't look like a giant marshmallow."

"Ahh, the ultimate dream. One can only hope." She squeezed his hand then let go and walked out of the room.

Atlas watched her go, wishing she was joining him with Gigi that morning. Shaking his head, he finished getting ready for the day and then went to find his grandmother.

"There you are," Aunt Patty said, looking relieved when Atlas arrived at his grandmother's bedroom door. "We've been waiting for you."

"Am I late?" he asked, moving toward the roaring fireplace to sit in the chair next to Gigi.

"No, honey," Gigi said, her voice barely audible just as Patty said, "Yes! Tim and I have errands. We'll be back later."

"Will you be here for—"

The door slammed and Aunt Patty was gone.

"She and Tim are dealing with the florist you hired for the wedding," Gigi said slowly, working hard to get the words out.

"Oh good. Did they get the flowers I special ordered for Payton?" Atlas asked. "They were supposed to be there this morning."

"They have. Patty's going to make sure the bouquets are made up the way you asked and then they'll bring everything back here. Patty said they'll take care of the remaining payment as a gift to you."

"They don't have to do that," he insisted.

"I know, but they want to. Don't fight them on this one."

"Fine. But they are getting a really great Christmas present."

"You always spoil everyone anyway." She smoothed the blanket that was covering her legs. "I have something for you, Alistair."

"You really didn't need to get me anything, Gigi. You know the greatest gift is just having you here with us."

"I know honey, but this is something you need." She pulled her hand out from beneath the blanket and opened her palm, revealing a familiar compass. "This was your grandfather's, you know."

He nodded. "Yes, he carried it with him everywhere. I thought you gave it to Uncle Tim."

"Timothy?" She shook her head. "No, this was never meant for him." Her watery blue eyes met his as she said, "Put your hand out."

Atlas did as he was told, knowing this was important. His grandfather hadn't gone a day in his life without that compass in his pocket. He'd never talked about it, but when he was stressed or upset, he'd take out the compass and hold it as if he were in prayer.

Gigi placed the cool gold piece in his palm and then curled his fingers around it. "This family compass is yours now, Alistair. Let this be your guiding light."

Warm light spilled through his fingers as it flashed over the gold case.

"Perfect," Gigi said, sounding more tired than usual. "The compass is now yours. Keep it safe."

Atlas stared at the compass in his hand. The magical light started to fade, but it was still warm to the touch. He glanced at Gigi. "I will, but are you sure you don't want to keep it? It was such a part of Grandpa that I think—"

"It's time for you to have it, Alistair." Her voice was firmer now, but her hands had started to shake. "It's what will guide you home."

He gave her a wry smile. "You know the stage is my home. I'm not sure I need the compass for that."

"The stage *has* been your home. That's true. But it won't be forever."

Gigi," he said, staring down at the glinting gold case of the compass. "Do you really think there will be a time when I won't be out on the road, sharing new work with the world?"

"Yes. And sooner than you think."

He frowned. "You're not trying to tell me to retire, are you? Because I can't imagine—"

"I'm not telling you to do anything, my darling boy. I'm just stating that at some point, your desire to be on that stage will wane. There's going to be somewhere else you want to be. The compass will guide you."

He didn't know what to make of any of that. For as long as he could remember, he'd been on a two-year cycle. Record music and then go out on tour. As soon as he got back, he'd start working on the next album.

"The future isn't written in stone, Alistair," she said quietly. "You have free will. But please, darling, promise me you'll listen when your heart speaks."

"I will," he said solemnly, since it appeared that she needed to hear his agreement.

"Good. That's good." She reached out to pat his arm. There were shadows under her eyes, and she was paler than usual.

"Gigi, do you need to lie down?" He was already on his feet, ready to help her move to the bed.

"I think I could use a bit of a nap."

Atlas didn't point out that it was only ten in the morning. Though inside, he was starting to freak out. The signs were there. Gigi's body was giving out on her. And no matter how strong her will was, there was nothing any of them could do to stop it. "I'll help you to the bed."

"Thank you, Alistair. I just need to close my eyes and—"

Gigi nodded off right there in the chair in front of the fireplace. Instead of waiting for someone to come help him, he just scooped up his grandmother and then gently laid her on the bed and pulled the throw over her body to keep her from getting chilled.

Then he pulled out the compass, wondering what it would do if he opened it. Would it point him back to the stage or to one of the houses he owned? He clutched it in his hand and decided it wasn't time to worry about it now. The only place that was home at the moment was the lake cabin because it housed all the people he cared about most.

He turned to leave but froze when he saw his brother Ashton standing in the doorway with his arms crossed over his chest. There was rage brewing in his eyes, and if Atlas hadn't known better, he'd have thought he was there to cause harm.

"Ashton, what's wrong?" he asked.

His brother stared pointedly at the compass in Atlas's hand. When Ashton raised his gaze to Atlas's, he slowly shook his head and sneered at the compass.

Before Atlas could ask him again what the issue was,

Ashton disappeared with a loud pop and a cloud of dark gray smoke.

"It looks like someone is going to have trouble dealing with change," Gigi said from her spot snuggled under the covers.

"No, he just... nothing has changed, Gigi."

"But it will, and he's not ready for it," his grandmother said.

"Are any of us?" Atlas asked.

"I am." She gave him a faint smile and then closed her eyes.

When her breathing evened out, Atlas grabbed his compass and left the room as quietly as when he'd come in.

CHAPTER 15

"Thank the gods," Payton whispered when she spotted Olivia in the room that had been designated the bridal suite.

Olivia hurried over to her and gave her a quick hug and a kiss on the cheek. "This is from Declan."

Payton glanced down at the brown paper bag and felt a smile tug at her lips. "Tell me it's his famous coffee cake."

She just shrugged.

"Don't play with me, Olivia," Payton teased as she opened the bag and lifted it to her nose. The sweet scent of sugar and spices filled her senses, and suddenly Payton's whole body started to relax. Her brother's coffee cake made everything better. "He's a god."

"Don't tell him that, or that ego of his will fill his entire kitchen," Olivia said as she sat on the loveseat that had been placed strategically in front of the mirrors where Payton would show off the day's selection of wedding dresses.

"Ha. He's not that bad. At least not when I'm around. It's a sister's job to keep her brother in check," Payton said and took a big bite of the pastry. "Oh. Em. Gee," she mumbled through the crumbs. "Delish."

"Omigiod, Payton!" Blake called out, sounding horrified. "What are you eating?"

Payton turned to look at the stylist who'd just walked in with a rolling garment rack full of wedding dresses. "Coffee cake. Want some?"

"No! You can't be eating that." She looked like she was about to hyperventilate.

"Why? My brother made it," Payton said as she and Olivia shared a confused look.

"Because you'll bloat, and then you won't fit into any of these dresses." She placed her hands on her hips and gave Payton a patronizing stare. "The sizing was already on the questionable side."

Olivia rolled her eyes.

"One piece of coffee cake doesn't mean I won't fit into those dresses." Payton stared at the stylist pointedly as she popped the last of the coffee cake into her mouth.

Blake pressed her lips together in a thin line and shook her head. "Don't say I didn't warn you." Then she stalked out of the room, muttering to herself about bridezillas.

"She's a little high strung," Olivia said.

Payton walked over to the rolling rack and started to look through the dresses. She knew from experience that most times the dresses looked very different when worn than they did while hanging, so she tried her best to remain positive. But when dress after dress after dress looked like it was straight from Amish country, she couldn't help but feel completely deflated.

"Payton, what's wrong?" Olivia asked, moving to stand next to her.

"Look at these. Is this what I told Blake I wanted yesterday?"

Olivia pulled one of the dresses off the rack and unzipped the plastic. The dress was completely plain, white with a high neckline and a straight body. The only detail was a lace collar that looked like it came straight from her grandmother's doily collection.

"You said elegant, not convent. What was that woman thinking?" Olivia asked in a hushed whisper.

Payton's eyes stung with frustrated tears, and she glanced away, embarrassed by her reaction. Why was she getting so emotional over a wedding dress for a fake wedding? It didn't make sense. Why did it matter what she wore?

She knew why it mattered.

Payton wanted to impress Atlas. She liked him, and even though she knew this would all be behind her soon, she didn't want to look back on the weekend and feel embarrassed by how she looked.

"There must be something better in here," Olivia said.

Payton turned and watched as her friend sorted through dress after dress.

When Olivia was done, her shoulders slumped, and she turned to Payton with a defeated expression. "Maybe she's still bringing things in?"

"At this point, I'd rather look like a cupcake than wear a white potato sack," Payton said.

Olivia grimaced.

The door swung open, and Blake strode back in with Alison on her heels. She was holding a couple more garment bags while Alison carried a tray with a carafe and mugs.

"Is that coffee?" Payton blurted. All she'd had that morning was the coffee cake. She needed something to wash it down. And maybe, just *maybe*, the caffeine in a cup of coffee would help her have a more positive outlook on the day. One could hope.

"It is." Alison grinned and set the tray on the table in front of the loveseat.

"Bless you," Payton said as she poured herself a cup and took a long sip of the rich liquid.

Olivia and Alison joined her while Blake busied herself reorganizing the dresses.

Payton was silent until Blake called her over and said, "Okay. I think we have the perfect thing for you today. Do you want to start with the full-length gowns or the knee-length ones?"

"Knee-length in December?" Payton asked. "Isn't the ceremony going to be outside?"

"Yes," Alison said. "On the dock. Hopefully with a fresh layer of snow. The pictures will be divine."

"Okay, no knee-length dresses. Would have been nice to know that yesterday," Blake muttered.

"You could have asked," Olivia said cheerfully.

Blake ignored her as she pushed back her long black hair. "All right, Payton. Let's just get started. Follow me."

Payton swallowed her protests and did as she was told. Five minutes later, she was on the pedestal, frowning at herself. The dress had no shape and nothing of interest other than the tiny string of pearls lining the neckline.

"What do we think?" Blake asked them, beaming as if she'd just unveiled a masterpiece.

No one said anything at first.

Finally, Olivia said, "I like how the sleeves hit just above the elbow, but they're really too tight, aren't they?"

The fit of the sleeves was the least of Payton's worries, but Olivia was right. She felt like she was going to lose circulation in her hands if she kept the dress on for much longer.

Blake *tsked.* "I told you not to eat that pastry."

"Seriously?" Payton snapped. "You think that coffee cake is going to make my arms swell or something?"

"It happens," she said, sounding defensive. "Since the dress isn't too form-fitting we just aren't noticing it anywhere else."

"Blake," Alison said with a shake of her head. "That's enough. Obviously, this dress is a no. Do you have anything that would be a flattering fit for Payton's shape? I'm picturing something with a V neckline, but not plunging, cinched at the waist with a skirt that flares out at the bottom. Maybe with some delicate lace lining it?"

"Yes, that sounds lovely," Payton said. "Did you bring anything like that? I like boat necklines, too, though."

"Um…" Blake tapped her chin as she stared off into the

distance. "Yeah, I'm sure I have something like that. Let me just…" She didn't finish her sentence as she disappeared back into the closet.

"No, I don't think she does," Olivia said. "Not unless she was holding it when she walked back in that last time."

Alison scrunched her nose as she looked in the direction of the closet. "You know, she came highly recommended by a friend of mine. I even flew her in for this. I'm sorry, Payton. This"—she waved at the potato sack dress Payton was wearing—"wasn't at all what I had in mind."

"Me either," Payton said, staring down at the plain white dress. "I could've made this with my own sewing machine."

"I'll be sure to tell the designer you said so," Blake said with a sniff, surprising Payton when she quietly came back into the room. "It's pretty obnoxious of you to assume you know better than an award-winning designer."

"Blake," Alison said with a voice of steel as she stood. "That's enough. Your job here is to find the perfect dress for the bride. Nothing more. Now, what have you found for Ms. McCabe?"

The stylist glared at Alison, clearly outraged that she'd been put in her place. But then she cleared her throat and produced another dress. This one was a baroque sheath dress with a matching waist-length jacket. "I think this one might give you the style and modesty you require."

"That's a choice," Olivia said, not bothering to hide her disapproval.

"It's very popular in certain circles," Blake said with a haughty expression.

"Which ones?" Payton asked. "Mother-of-the-bride circles? Or assisted living homes?"

Olivia snorted out a laugh.

Alison just stared in confusion. "Uh, while that is a lovely fabric, Blake, don't you think it's more suited for an older bride? In fact, I think my grandmother wore something similar to my aunt's recommitment ceremony a few years back."

"Style is timeless," Blake said with a sniff of superiority.

"Okay," Alison said with a frown. "But that's nothing like what I described, so I'm not sure why you're showing it to us. I don't even know why you brought it. It's definitely not something Payton would wear or that she asked for. Look at her. Her style is understated class. This is... I don't know, dated and far too modest. She said she wanted more modest than what you showed us yesterday, not something that would be suitable for the minister's wife. Goddess above, she's marrying a rock star. Give her something to work with!"

Payton wanted to pump her fist in the air and then applaud Alison's speech. But when she looked at Blake, she noticed the woman's face had turned bright red, and she looked like her head might explode.

"I brought rock star-edgy dresses yesterday," Blake thundered. "I was told that none of them were suitable and that she wanted more modest dresses. So I *brought* modest dresses, and now you're telling me these aren't good enough either? You people need to make up your minds. I don't have unlimited time, you know. I can't believe I gave up going to London for this. I haven't even gotten an autograph from Atlas yet."

"You brought dresses that were more fitting for the MTV awards yesterday," Alison said. "My sister-in-law isn't going to walk down the aisle in front of my grandmother with her junk hanging out. Whatever happened to classic elegance?"

"You only gave me forty-eight hours to pull this off. And she's not even a sample size. I did the best I could!" Blake was vibrating with frustration now.

"I think we're done here," Alison told Blake. "Gather your dresses and go. You're no longer needed."

"What?" the stylist asked, pressing her hand to her chest, her eyes wide with shock. "You can't fire me. We have a contract."

"I can and I will." Alison pulled her phone out of her skirt pocket and send a text. When she was done, she glared at the other woman. "Maybe you can still make that flight to London."

If Payton hadn't known better, she'd have bet money that steam was going to come out of Blake's ears. The woman was so angry her entire body was shaking.

"Take that dress off," Blake ordered Payton. "And don't stain it like you did the other one."

"Stain?" Payton asked. "I didn't—"

"You did. One of the dresses from yesterday now has pit stains. I'll tell the designer to send you the bill," she snarled before she stomped back into the closet.

"That's not true," Payton said, turning to Alison. "I was freezing most of the day because I was half naked."

Alison waved a hand as if dismissing the entire idea. "Don't worry about it. If she does send a bill, just forward it to me. I'll handle her."

Payton nodded and turned so that Olivia could help her out of the dress. Once she was back in her own clothes, she brought the dress to the closet to give to Blake.

Just as she reached the doorway, she heard a string of curses and then a loud crash from inside.

Payton hurried into the closet to find Blake trapped under the rolling rack.

"Help!" Blake called and then her eyes widened in horror. "Oh my goddess, no! Stop them!"

"Stop who?" Payton asked, already tugging the rack back onto its wheels. She crouched down and held out a hand to help the stylist.

"Leave me," Blake ordered as she pushed herself up to her hands and knees. "Go save the dresses!"

Payton finally followed Blake's horrified expression and let out a gasp when she spotted two gray kittens clawing at one of the dresses and a black and white one hanging from the bodice of another.

"Olivia! Alison!" Payton called as she ran over to pluck the black and white kitten off the nearest dress.

She heard the other two women rush in, and as she reached for another kitten, she handed the black and white one off to Olivia.

"Where did these cats come from?" Alison demanded.

Payton retrieved one of the gray kittens easily, but the other one darted under one of the skirts and scrambled up the inside of the dress, making it difficult for Payton to reach it.

"Here, give me that one," Olivia said from behind her.

Payton didn't hesitate. She relinquished the cat and then turned the wedding dress around to unzip it. The kitten scrambled again, leaving claw marks in the delicate silk fabric. Payton winced, but she reached in and finally got the squirming kitten under her control.

When she turned around, both Olivia and Alison were staring at the stylist in disbelief.

"What's going on? Did you bring these kittens with you today?" Payton asked.

Blake pressed her fingers to her temple as she slowly shook her head.

It was then that Payton noticed the red-tinged magic sparking from her fingertips.

"Did you summon these kittens?" Payton asked. "They weren't here before when I was in here. Or if they were, they—"

"She didn't summon them," Alison said, her voice flat. "She had a fit when I fired her, and she was so angry that her magic got away from her and literally produced them out of thin air."

"As in, she was so mad she *had kittens*?" Olivia asked with a bark of laughter.

"That's what it looks like to me." Alison pointed at the two kittens snuggling in Olivia's arms. "See how they still have traces of her red-tinged magic clinging to them?"

"Look," Blake said, blowing out a breath as tears filled

her dark eyes. "I can't help it if I got upset. It's not like I meant to summon them. It just... happened."

"Now you get to tell the designers that you had a temper tantrum, and your new kittens destroyed their dresses," Alison said.

"They aren't my kittens," Blake said, backing away as she held her hands up. "I'm allergic. That's why I didn't help Payton retrieve them. If I touch them, my eyes will be watering for hours."

"You've got to be freakin' kidding me." Alison pinched the bridge of her nose. "Just gather what's left of this mess and go before you ruin anything else."

Payton and Olivia retreated to the bedroom with their cute little charges and waited until Blake was finally gone.

Alison flopped down into the chair across from them and blew out a long breath. "That did not go well."

"But we have three really cute little kittens," Payton said, scratching one of the gray ones behind the ear. It leaned into her and started to purr.

"Oh no, don't remind me. What are we going to do with kittens? And I very much doubt the owners of the cabin are going to be pleased if they find out we have three furry squatters here."

"I can probably take one," Olivia said, holding the other gray one up and nuzzling it with her nose. "My dog, Apollo, might balk a little bit, but he'll get used to this little cutie soon enough."

"That's a start, I guess." Alison leaned back in the chair and stared up at the ceiling. "I'm sure we'll figure out what to do with the kittens. But what are we going to do about a wedding dress? It's two days before the wedding, and we have nothing for the bride to wear."

Payton shrugged. "Atlas and I made a deal that we'd both just wear jeans if I didn't find something great to wear. I'm down for that." In fact, she wasn't just down, she was relieved. If she had to try on one more hideous wedding dress, she might just break out into hives.

"Payton," Alison said, her tone incredulous. "You cannot wear jeans. I don't care what Atlas says. That is just not going to happen. Not on my watch." She turned her focus to Olivia. "Are there any bridal boutiques in town?"

"Yes, it's called Noel's Bridal, but I'm pretty sure she's open by appointment only due to the season. The most popular time to get married in Christmas Grove is December, so dresses get ordered in the spring. Right now, it's just pickups and alterations."

"Then I'll get an appointment." Alison met Payton's eyes. "Don't you worry about a thing. I'll fix this."

"Okay," Payton said, fully believing her. She'd never seen a more determined person.

It took Alison less than a minute to get Noel on the phone. When she ended the call, she beamed. "Noel is headed to the shop now. Olivia, do you have time to help me pick out a few dresses for Payton?"

"Sure, but why doesn't Payton just go with us?" Olivia asked.

"I can—" Payton started.

But Alison cut her off. "Payton has an appointment in thirty minutes with Atlas to pick the cake. She can't go."

"Oh," Payton said, sinking back into her chair. For a

minute there, she was a bit excited about having a store full of dresses to choose from. But Olivia wouldn't let her down. She knew whatever her friend brought back would work just fine, so why did Payton feel a tiny pang of loss over not being able to pick out her own wedding dress?

"Are you okay?" Olivia asked as they left the room.

Payton nodded. "Sure. I get to taste cake and play with kittens." She wrinkled her nose as she added, "You, on the other hand, have to go shopping during Christmas season. Good luck."

Olivia patted her arm, and for some reason, even though Olivia didn't say anything, Payton was certain that she could see right through her.

CHAPTER 16

"Where did these little fuzzballs come from?" Danny asked when he appeared in the great room wearing black jeans and a green button-down shirt. Olivia and Alison had just left after the three of them got the kittens tucked into a large cardboard box with a blanket.

Payton looked up at Atlas's handsome cousin and said, "The stylist had literal kittens when Alison fired her. Turns out her magic went haywire, and these little cutie pies showed up. Then they tried to destroy a couple of dresses, but that's beside the point."

"The stylist had literal kittens?" he parroted. Then he threw his head back and laughed. When he regained control of himself, he took a seat on the floor next to Payton and added, "That's the best thing I've heard all month."

"It was something. Anyway, now we're stuck with three

kittens who need homes because Blake bolted and refused to deal with her mess."

"Aww, finding them homes shouldn't be an issue." He reached into the box and pulled out the black and white one. After a quick check of her kitty parts, he said, "What should we name this little girl?"

"Bells," Payton said. "You know, like jingle bells."

"Perfect. And these other two?" he asked.

"I think my friend is going to take that one." She pointed to the gray one with a white nose. "So I'll let Olivia name her. As for the other one... boy or girl?"

"Boy," Danny said after violating the kitty's privacy.

"St. Nick," Payton decided.

"Danny, are you flirting with my wife?" Atlas asked, appearing suddenly.

"Nope, but I am falling in love with these kittens." Danny held the black and white one up. "This is Bells. And the one your bride is holding has been named St. Nick."

Atlas came to stand behind Payton and peered into the box. "You forgot one."

Payton chuckled and then explained Olivia had already claimed it and now they had a mission to find homes for the other two.

"Not yet, you won't," Gigi said from somewhere in the room, her voice trembling.

Atlas turned, exposing her to Payton. The older woman was leaning on a walker and looked a little out of breath. "Gigi," Atlas said, hurrying to her side. "You should have texted me. I'd have come to help you."

"Don't coddle me, Alistair. Sometimes an old woman

just wants to do things for herself. Now if you want to help me, you'll bring me one of those kittens to love on."

"On it." Atlas took the kitten that Payton held out for him and returned quickly to his grandmother's side. "Do you want to hold him?"

"No," Gigi said. "Just let me pet him for a minute before I take a seat." She looked over at Payton. "Who do these kittens belong to?"

"Me, I guess," Payton said with a grimace. She once again explained the kitten debacle, and by the time she finished, Gigi was laughing and shaking her head in disbelief.

"I told Alison to do a reference check on that stylist," Gigi said, shaking her head. "She's too trusting, but I won't be sorry about the kittens. They're just too sweet." She scratched St. Nick under his chin before clutching her walker again. "Alistair, can you please help me to my chair?"

"Of course."

Once she was situated, she reached out for St. Nick. Atlas handed the kitten to her, and all of them watched as she lovingly doted on the animal.

The pure joy on Gigi's face was enough to make Payton forgive Blake for her outburst as well as leaving the kittens. Anything that put that sweet smile on Atlas's face as he watched his grandmother was worth all the trouble in the world.

The doorbell rang, and Atlas went to answer it before Payton could even get to her feet. She hurried after Atlas, wondering what she was going to be blindsided with next. But when Atlas waved in a woman who was wearing a chef's coat and carrying two large pastry boxes, she remembered that they were supposed to do the cake tasting.

"Please tell me you're hungry," Payton said as they followed the pastry chef into the cabin's spacious kitchen.

"Why? Are we having a donut picnic?" he asked, his eyes glinting with amusement.

"No donuts here, sir," the woman deadpanned. "I hope you like cake, because you're about to taste about a dozen different varieties."

He nodded. "I definitely like cake, just as long as it doesn't have coconut in it. I'm allergic."

The chef raised her head and stared at him with interest. Then she frowned. "Are you sure?"

"Yes, I'm sure. It's severe enough that I carry an epi pen with me everywhere I go. Especially since a lot of places are starting to use coconut instead of almond milk." Atlas took a seat at the table that had a clear view of his grandmother and the kitten in the other room. "Otherwise, I'll pretty much try anything once."

"Okay then." The chef gave him a decisive nod and got to work unpacking the cake samples.

Payton took a seat next to Atlas and asked, "How was your morning?"

"Good. I had a nice visit with Gigi before her nap. Then I went for a short walk around the property and might have wished you were there. The fresh layer of snow was spectacular, especially with all the sunshine today."

"I would have liked that," she said, brushing a lock of hair back as she watched the beautiful man sitting next to her. "I bet it's pretty rare for anyone to see you in your natural habitat."

He chuckled. "Isn't my natural habitat the stage?"

"No. I saw you last night under the stars. You really like the outdoors. I bet that's where you go when you need to think something over or just want a little peace."

"You're spot on," Gigi said from her chair in the other room. "He commands the stage, but it's not where he recharges. He does that out in the sunshine and under the moon."

Payton nodded, feeling a bit proud of herself. "See?" she whispered as she leaned toward him. "I learn fast."

"You guessed," Atlas said, but the light in his eyes told her that he'd appreciated being seen.

"Does it matter? How about we take a walk this afternoon to work off the cake. Blake says if I eat anything remotely fun I'm going to bloat."

"Blake? The stylist my sister fired?" he asked, frowning.

"Yes. How'd you know about that?" Payton hadn't talked to him about the stylist yet.

"Alison called. She wanted to update me."

The chef placed a tasting plate in front of each of them and asked, "Is anyone else sitting in on this tasting? We have enough for five or six people." She checked her notes in her pocket. "Yes, the order was for five samples of each cake."

"That must have been so we could include Olivia and Alison," Payton said. "Unfortunately, they aren't here. But Danny is." She turned her attention to the man who was still entertaining two of the kittens. "Want to join us?"

"For cake? Hell, yeah." He placed Bells back in the

makeshift kitty bed, and then instead of leaving it on the floor, he picked up the box and brought it with him into the kitchen. "I don't want them to get lonely."

"It looks like those kittens already found a father," Atlas whispered.

"It does, doesn't it?" she said, feeling light and happy just as she had the night before. There was something about Atlas that just made all her stress fade away. She didn't know how he did it, or if he even knew he was doing it. All she wanted was to spend as much time with him as possible so she'd remember that perfect feeling.

"Okay, first round," the chef said, placing something in front of them that looked like it should be named Death by Chocolate.

The three of them tasted, moaned, and then rated the cake on scoring cards the chef had left for each of them.

"That was incredible," Payton said, ready to scratch her own eyeballs out. The woman had skills that Payton only dreamed of.

"Wait until you try this one," the chef said as she placed slices of cake in front of them that filled the room with a rich coffee aroma.

"Oh, holy hell balls," Atlas said, mumbling through the bite he was savoring.

"I concur." Payton even licked her plate when the chef wasn't watching. It was that good.

A few minutes later, the chef looked at Payton and Danny and said, "This one has coconut, so I'm putting it away unless the two of you want to try it."

"No thanks," Payton said. She didn't care for coconut anyway.

Danny eyed the cake, looking more than a little interested.

"Go on," Payton urged. "It's already paid for, so don't let it go to waste.

They went through another half a dozen cakes, each of them as delicious as the first few.

"How are we going to decide?" Payton asked Atlas. "Do you have a favorite?"

He opened his mouth to speak, but the chef cut him off. "There's just one more. Don't make any judgments until you've tried this, a true specialty."

"Far be it from me not to give a cake it's due process," Atlas said.

Payton snorted. "Due process? It's a cake, dude."

"An important one, apparently," he said, grinning.

The three of them were having too much fun to even notice when the last plate was served. Payton had missed whatever the chef had called it. It looked like some sort of carrot cake, and Payton dug in.

She closed her eyes, trying to decipher the flavor profile. Vanilla, honey, cinnamon, nutmeg, and—"

Payton didn't think at all when she turned and smacked Atlas to keep him from eating the cake. *Whack!* The cake, as well as the plate and a fork, went flying and clattered to the floor.

"Ouch! What was that for?" Atlas practically growled at her.

"It had coconut in it," she said, trying to reach up and

soothe the red mark she'd left on his face. "I didn't want you to die."

Payton wished the floor would open up and swallow her whole after she smacked Atlas, but what other choice had she had? None. "I'm sorry. Are you all right?"

"I'm better than all right," he said, draping his arm around her shoulders and pulling her in so that he could plant a kiss on her temple. "I'm the one who should be thanking you. The alternative is that I'd be laid out for at least twenty-four hours and end up with an epinephrine hangover."

Payton glared at the chef. "I thought you said you only had one cake with coconut in it."

The chef was suddenly flustered as she reviewed her notes. Her lips moved, but no sound came out as she read the cards. Finally, her lips stopped moving and her face turned pale. "Oh no. I'm so sorry, Mr. Mazer. It was a mistake. One that could have been deadly," she said as if he didn't already know that. "Please accept my apologies. I've never done that before, and we work with allergies all the time. I think maybe I'm just a little starstruck. You know, rock star and all."

She'd been starstruck? Payton found that hard to believe. The woman had been almost robotic the entire time. But when Atlas got up to go over and talk to her, the chef's face flushed deep red when Atlas gave her a hug. "It's okay," he said. "My wife saved the day." Atlas blew Payton a kiss, and she decided it really wasn't the chef's fault. It was just that disorienting being around such a beautiful and charming man.

CHAPTER 17

"*W*e're back!" Alison called as she and Olivia strode through the front door of the cabin.

Payton looked up from where she was playing with Bells and tried to swallow her anxiety. Her last two rounds of trying on dresses had been so awful she couldn't help the nervousness that was gripping her body. Why couldn't they have just gone along with her plans to wear jeans?

"Don't look so panicked," Olivia said with a reassuring smile. "We got it. I promise."

"Let's hope so," Payton said, unable to relax. This dress debacle was really messing with her head. She turned to Atlas, who was sitting next to her. "You'll take care of the kittens?"

"Oh, we brought kitty supplies, too," Alison said before her brother could answer. "They're in the rental. Atlas, would you be a dear and go get them?"

"I'll do it," Danny said, already heading for the door.

"Such a helpful young man," Gigi said. She was tucked under a blanket at the end of the couch in front of the fireplace. Her color was a little better than it had been earlier in the day. Payton thought it had to do with the kittens. She hadn't stopped petting the one in her lap since the moment she was settled.

"He is," Atlas agreed. "Sure, Pay. I'll take care of these guys. Go do your thing."

She leaned over and gave him a kiss on his cheek. The same one she'd ended up smacking during the cake tasting, and she said a silent thank you that the red mark had disappeared.

"Aww, if that isn't the sweetest thing," Alison mocked and then pretended to gag.

Payton couldn't help the laugh that tumbled from her lips. It was exactly how she behaved with her own brother. The dynamics were comforting in an otherwise slightly awkward situation.

"It *is* sweet, Alison," Atlas shot back. "You'd know that if you weren't so busy busting my balls all the time."

His sister just smirked at him and then gestured for Payton to follow her.

Once they were back in the designated bridal suite, a room Payton would be happy never to see again, Olivia said, "We have two dresses. One is the right size, and I think it's going to be the perfect fit. It's a nice dress, but we both agree that it's probably not *the* dress."

"I'm sure it's fine," Payton said, trying to be pragmatic. "As long as it's stylish and actually covers my body without swallowing me whole, then we'll be in great shape."

"Sure, but we also found a gown that we both think is perfect for you," Alison added. "It's just that it's two sizes too big. So we brought it back for you to try on to see if you love the dress. If so, we can get the right size overnighted from Noel's sister shop up in Befana Bay, Washington."

"Okay, let's do this," Payton said. "The one that's supposed to fit first." She really just wanted a dress that would work. The sooner that was done, the sooner the sinking feeling in her stomach would go away. At least she hoped so.

Olivia and Alison both disappeared into the closet. A few moments later, they both reappeared with Olivia holding a pretty satin dress with lace overlay. It had cap sleeves, a sweetheart neckline, and a slit to mid-thigh in the flowing skirt.

"That's really pretty," Payton said, relieved. It was definitely a dress she could happily wear without feeling like she was cosplaying as someone else.

"It is, isn't it?" Olivia helped her get into the dress. Once it was zipped and buttoned in the back, Olivia turned her around so she could see herself in the mirror.

There was no question that the lacy white dress was gorgeous. And it was a bonus that it was the perfect fit. But when she slipped her hands into the pockets and bent her knee, showing off the slit, she just didn't connect with it. If she were trying it on at a store, she'd think maybe the dress was trying too hard with the lace and the slit.

"It's a gorgeous dress," Alison said from behind her.

Payton nodded. "It really is. Anyone would be lucky to wear it on their big day."

"You don't like it," Olivia said. It was a statement, not a question.

"It's not that I don't like it. I do. It's miles better than anything Blake brought here. It's just... I don't know. Maybe a little too fussy for me with the lace. But it is really lovely."

"I thought you'd say that," Olivia said with a sharp nod. "Okay, it's a decent backup, but let's try the other dress. If you like it, we need to call Noel right away to get the smaller one shipped."

Alison disappeared into the closet to retrieve the highly anticipated dress while Payton stepped out of the first option. When she returned, Payton took one look at the dress in her hands and knew it was going to be the winner. The simple and modern elegance was exactly her style.

It took a little bit of work to get Payton into the second dress. Because it was two sizes too big, they had to clip the fabric together on the sides and in the back in order to show what Payton would look like in the correctly sized dress.

"Oh my," Olivia said in a hushed tone when she stepped back to get a good look at Payton. Tears filled her eyes, and she let out a tiny laugh. "Sorry, it's just... perfect."

"It really is," Alison said, looking pleased with herself. Atlas's sister grabbed her phone and took a quick picture. "You're going to want this for the memory book."

Payton finally turned and stared at herself in the mirror. She knew instantly this was *her* dress. The one she should get married in. For half a second, she wondered if she should wear the other dress and save this one for whenever the big day actually did happen, but she quickly nixed that idea. When she pictured herself walking down the aisle to Atlas, she could only envision herself in this dress.

She had to have it.

The simple satin dress was backless with a deep V neckline. It was cinched at the waist, with a thick, folded band of the same fabric that gave it texture and interest. But possibly her favorite part was the wrap-around skirt. It had just enough volume to make her feel beautiful, but it wasn't so over the top that she felt as if she were drowning in fabric.

"Call Noel," Payton said. "This is it."

"I'm on it," Alison said, beaming as she tapped at her phone and then pressed it to her ear. "Noel? We're going to need that dress." There was a slight pause before she continued. "Yes, just use the credit card on file. Thank you."

"Payton," Olivia said, standing behind her and staring in the mirror. "You look like a million bucks in this dress." She lowered her voice to barely a whisper as she added, "Atlas isn't ever gonna want to let you go."

An intense longing gripped Payton, one she'd never felt before for anyone, much less a man she barely knew. But it was right there, and there was no sense in denying it. She wanted Atlas Mazer. Not because he was a rich, gorgeous musician, but because of who he was underneath the famous rock star.

He'd been nothing but attentive, respectful, and most importantly, the kind of man whose heart was bigger than the moon. She'd thought he was crazy to concoct a scheme to pretend to be married, but after just a few days, it was obvious Atlas would do anything for his family. His love was pure, and in her experience, that kind of heart was very rare.

The way he sat with Gigi each day, giving her his undivided attention and showing her just how much she was loved, had touched Payton deep in her soul.

She was in too deep already. There was no doubt about it; parting ways with him was going to wound her. But one thing was for sure, she knew she'd carry a piece of him with her for the rest of her life.

CHAPTER 18

"*I* think that kitten is distracting you." Atlas teased his grandmother as he won another game of cribbage. His grandfather had taught him to play when he was just a boy, and after he'd passed on, he and his grandmother had played as a way of remembering him. Most days, Gigi beat him. But today, she was too enamored with the kitten that Payton had named St. Nick. "This is the second game in a row that I've won."

"Oh, Alistair, haven't you learned already that I only *let* you win?" she teased back before lifting the kitten to give him a kiss on his nose.

He chuckled. "You have never let anyone win a game of anything a day in your life. Don't try to gaslight me just because you're more interested in St. Nick than you are me and this game."

She gave him her signature side-eye, making him laugh harder.

"Fine. You let me win. Are you going to let me win again, or are you ready for something else?"

"We can keep playing," she said, reaching for the deck even though both her hands were shaking. He frowned and opened his mouth to suggest she get some rest, but before he could speak, she said, "Don't try to manage me, Alistair. I'm exactly where I want to be, doing what I want to do."

"Yes, ma'am," he said with a salute. "But at least let me shuffle those for you so you can spoil that cat some more."

She paused for a moment and then nodded. "Okay, but I'm keeping my eye on you."

Atlas shook his head. "Have I ever tried to cheat at cards before?"

"There's a first time for everything." She gave him a tiny wink before turning her attention back to the kitten.

"We made it!" Aunt Patty called from the foyer. She poked her head into the great room. "Oh, there you are. Atlas, can we get some help? The rental is jam-packed."

"Sure." He leaned over and gave Gigi a kiss on the cheek. "I'll be back. Do you need anything? Water? Tea? Cookies?"

"Oh, now you did it. There are cookies?" she asked, her eyes lighting with interest.

"There are. I'll grab you one before I go help Patty and Tim."

"Thanks, love. St. Nick needs a treat, too."

"I wouldn't dream of leaving him out." He quickly found one of the store-bought Christmas cookies and made a mental note to ask Payton if they could make some homemade ones before the weekend was over. Then he found the kitty treats with the rest of the supplies Alison had gotten earlier and delivered them to Gigi, who beamed at him.

He squeezed her hand briefly and went out into the cold to help his uncle, who was hauling what looked like an entire floral shop out of the SUV. He clapped Tim on the back. "Where are we putting these?"

"There's a workshop off the garage that's climate controlled. I'll lead." Tim hit a button that opened one of the garage doors. "This way."

A half hour later, Atlas and Tim made their way back into the house just as Olivia was leaving with the yet-to-be-named kitten in her arms. Alison was on her phone again while Payton was saying her goodbyes. The moment she saw Atlas though, her eyes lit up and she gave him a flirty little wave.

He walked right up to her, grabbed her around the waist, and gave her a chaste but lingering kiss.

"Whoa," Olivia said softly.

When Atlas released Payton, he noted Olivia's moony-eyed expression and stood a little taller, feeling please with himself.

"That was unexpected," Payton whispered.

"Should I have kept my distance?"

"No," she said immediately and then flushed. "I was just caught a little off guard is all. Next time I won't be."

"Next time. I like the sound of that."

Olivia cleared her throat. "Uh, I don't mean to interrupt, but what time should Declan and I be here on Sunday?"

Payton looked up at Atlas. "The ceremony is at two, right?"

"Yep."

She turned back to Olivia. "Noon. I'm gonna need you to help me get ready."

"You got it." She leaned in and hugged Payton and then nodded at Atlas. "See you both on Sunday." She opened the door, paused, and looked over her shoulder. "Have fun in the meantime, both of you."

Payton nodded and then turned to Atlas once she was gone. "Okay, anything else on the schedule today?"

"You heard Olivia. Fun. How about it? We could take a walk, maybe make a snowman."

"Or snowwoman," she said.

He chuckled. "How about a snow family?"

"I'm in."

To his surprise, she slipped her hand into his. He tightened his grip and heard a voice in the back of his head say, *Don't let this one go.*

I don't plan on it, he thought and then tugged Payton toward the garage. "I've got something to show you first."

"This isn't an *I'll show you mine if you show me yours* type of situation, is it?" Payton asked.

Atlas blinked at her and then gave her a slow grin. "It wasn't, but it could be if that's what you want."

"You're too easy," she said, lightly punching his arm. "Come on. What do you really want me to see?"

He cast a suggestive glance down at his body, not willing to let her comment slide that easily. He loved playful Payton, and he would do everything he could to bring out that side of her.

"Oh. Em. Gee. Don't make me regret flirting with you," she said, shaking her head and laughing.

"You don't regret a thing, and you know it." He grabbed her hand again and led the way out to the workshop.

The moment they stepped inside the cool room, Payton let out a small gasp. "Red and white sunflowers?" She grabbed Atlas's arm. "Who picked these?"

"I did." He gave her a self-satisfied smile. "I might have asked around about your favorite flower. With it being the holiday season, the florist talked me into the white and red ones. I hope you're not disappointed there's no yellow."

"Are you kidding?" she asked with tears in her eyes. "But how? The local florist wouldn't have these this time of year."

"I had them flown in." He tried to keep the smugness out of his tone. But the truth was, he'd put in a significant amount of effort to get those flowers as soon as she'd agreed to the surprise wedding his family had orchestrated. He'd wanted to do something to show his appreciation. It looked like it was a success.

"You're incredible. When did you do this?"

He shrugged. "Yesterday, right after my family sprung this on us."

"That means you had them overnighted from somewhere."

"Perhaps." It had taken quite a bit of cajoling and a heavy surcharge, but in the end, he'd gotten what he wanted. When one had money, it was less of an issue turning a firm no into a yes.

"That's... insane. They're just perfect, Atlas. Thank you.

It's exactly what I would have picked for a December wedding. I can't believe you did this."

"Why not?" he asked, a little offended. "It's the least I could do after you agreed to marry me this weekend."

She finally tore her gaze away from the flowers and gave him her full attention. "It's just that no one, not even the guy I dated for a few years, has ever done something this thoughtful for me. Fake or not, somehow this is turning out to be my dream wedding."

He couldn't help the next words that slipped out of his mouth. "If only we could overnight your dream guy, too."

She swept her gaze over him as her tongue darted out to moisten her lips. The small movement made him want to back her up against the wall and claim her mouth with his. Bury his hands in her hair and show her exactly how much he wanted her.

"There's no need to overnight him," she said, her gaze now firmly on his. "Not when he's standing right in front of me."

Oh damn. Did she really just say that? Yes. Yes, she did. Atlas didn't hesitate. He moved in, cupped both of her cheeks, and took her mouth, claiming her for his own.

Payton met his kiss with a fervor of her own, fueling his need for her.

Atlas turned her, pressing her up against a nearby cabinet, and groaned when their bodies molded together. He wanted to touch her everywhere, explore every inch of her body with just his lips. The world fell away, and all he could focus on were her delicate fingers slipping underneath his shirt to touch his burning flesh.

Following her lead, he caressed the exposed skin at her waistline and nearly lost his mind when she bit down gently on his lower lip.

He let out a growl and went for her neck, nipping and sucking and—

"My eyes!" Alison called from somewhere across the workshop.

Payton jerked back, tugging her shirt back into place. "Alison, we were just, um..."

"It's obvious what you were doing, Payton," Alison said, chuckling to herself. "Honestly, with you guys being newlyweds, I'm surprised I haven't walked in on more of this activity."

"What are you doing in here, Alison? Do you need something?" Atlas asked, more than a little annoyed. Leave it to his sister to interrupt just when things were getting heated.

"Yes, as a matter of fact, I do. Gigi is ready for dinner. It's been a busy day, so I thought we'd just order something. There's a place called Apollo's that looks like it has a great pasta selection. Does that sound good?"

Payton laughed.

"What's funny?" Alison asked, looking confused.

"Payton and her brother own Apollo's," Atlas said.

"Sorry, yes. My brother is the chef there," Payton said with a smirk. "We can order if you want, but it'd be faster, fresher, and better if you let me make it."

"Better?" Atlas asked with a raised eyebrow. "Is this a sibling rivalry I'm hearing?"

"Damned straight. Every time Declan and I have a cook-off, I win. He's a good chef, but I'm better. It's my earth magic. He can't compete with that."

"I see." Alison patted her brother's arm. "I'm better than Atlas at pretty much everything, too. I just let him have the music thing so he doesn't get a complex."

Atlas rolled his eyes but opted to let her statement go. She was only trying to bait him.

Alison ignored him. "Anyway, I don't want you to have to cook. It's your wedding weekend. You should be relaxing and enjoying yourself, not stuck in the kitchen all weekend."

"I don't feel stuck," Payton said. "Honestly, the reason I'm a chef is because I love it. I told you before that I enjoy cooking, so it's really not a burden at all."

"Only if you're sure," Alison said, chewing on her bottom lip.

"I'm sure. Let's go in so I can get started. Gigi's waiting."

CHAPTER 19

"So, Chef Payton, what are we making?" Atlas asked as he tied on an apron with a picture of a melting snowman. *If you can't take the heat, stay out of the kitchen* was printed across the top.

"Mediterranean chicken linguini with sundried tomatoes, spinach, and capers." Payton pulled out a cutting board and got to work on slicing the thawed chicken. "There's also a loaf of artisan bread in there. I thought we'd warm it up and serve it with the pasta."

"All of that sounds delicious, Payton," Alison said. "Seriously, my mouth is already watering."

"It won't take long." Payton waved a hand toward the great room. "Have a seat. Atlas and I can handle this."

"Are you sure?" Alison asked, eyeing her brother. "I'm pretty sure the only thing Atlas knows how to do in the kitchen is reheat takeout containers."

"She's not wrong," Atlas admitted. "But I'm pretty sure I can take direction."

Alison snorted on her way into the great room.

"I think she has reservations," Payton said, smirking at Atlas. "How about you start with setting the table?"

"On it." Atlas took care of the table while Payton got the pasta cooking and sautéed the chicken and spinach. She was so engrossed in making sure she timed everything right that she didn't pay any attention to Atlas until he peered over her shoulder to inspect her cooking.

"Do you need something, rock star?" she asked.

"Yes. Praise for setting the table."

"You can't be that needy." She opened the oven and slid the bread in. After setting the timer, she glanced at Atlas. "Did you put the butter out?"

"I did," he said, drumming his chest with his fist as if he'd just conquered something.

"Glasses?"

"Yep."

"Olive oil and balsamic vinegar?"

"Um, what?" he asked, blinking at her like she was speaking a foreign language.

She chuckled. "I guess you didn't quite scale that mountain."

"Fine," he said. "You got me. Tell me what we need the oil and vinegar for."

"The bread. And it's extra virgin olive oil and balsamic vinegar. The distinction matters." When she was done sautéing the chicken, she set it aside with the spinach and turned her attention to her fake husband. "Grab four small plates and bring them over here."

After he did as she said, she showed him how to combine the oil and vinegar and then added a dash of rosemary for flavor. "This is for dipping the bread. It's delicious."

"It smells like it," he said, sounding impressed.

"You're too easy," she said as she took the pasta off the stove.

"Easy? Wanna find out?" he asked suggestively.

It was on the tip of her tongue to say yes, but instead she pretended she didn't hear him. She was already having enough issues resisting this man. If they kept flirting shamelessly, she'd end up right back in his arms with no thought in her head other than how much she wanted him.

That wasn't a good plan.

If she wanted to make it out of the weekend without her heart shattered, she'd need to maintain some sort of self-control. Though she didn't know what she was going to do when she had to climb back into bed with him. After that make-out session in the workshop, she didn't know how she was going to be able to keep her hands to herself. Maybe she'd stay up reading until he fell asleep. Or she'd take a long bath. Or throw herself in the lake to cool herself off.

Yeah. That was it. A dip in the freezing lake would snuff the fire out.

Gods, she sure hoped so.

The timer on the stove sounded, indicating the bread was warm. A few minutes later, Payton set the food on the table and called, "Dinner's ready."

The meal was an enjoyable affair. The entire family was there, with Gigi at the head of the table. Payton, Atlas, and Alison were on one side, while Patty, Tim, and Danny were on the other.

"This is delicious, Payton," Danny said, reaching for a second helping of the pasta. "Atlas is a lucky man."

"True," Atlas agreed. "But I helped. I made this amazing dipping oil." He puffed his chest out, acting as if he'd invented the concept of olive oil and balsamic vinegar.

"Brilliant," Danny deadpanned.

Everyone laughed, and the talk turned to Atlas's plans for the next year. He caught Payton's eye and said, "Spend time with my wife. Write music. Learn to blow glass."

"You, a glassblower? Alison asked, looking surprised. "I've never heard you mention that before."

"It's just something I've been thinking about," Atlas said.

"Now that's something I'd like to see you try. If you do, let me know, and I'll do it with you," Danny said and then stuffed his mouth full of pasta.

"Yeah, I'd do it too," Alison said. "But only if you promise to show up. I'm tired of making plans and then having them canceled when the label calls because they booked you for a last-minute gig. Then there's that whole thing where you blow me off to write more songs." Alison turned to Payton. "That's what he did for my last birthday. We were supposed to take a trip to New York, and he canceled on me last minute. Said he had songs to write that couldn't wait."

Atlas winced and averted his gaze. His face was flushed, and he started to drum his fingers on the table.

Payton had the distinct impression it wasn't Atlas that

couldn't wait to write the songs. It sounded to her a lot more like maybe his twin had things to say. She patted his arm and then covered his hand with hers. "We'll see how it goes."

"Just don't get mad and dump his workaholic butt," Danny said. "I'd really miss your kitchen skills for these family events."

"It's nice to be appreciated," she said with a soft chuckle.

"Dude, my wife isn't your personal chef," Atlas grumbled.

Danny rolled his eyes but didn't bother to reply. There was no need. Everyone but Atlas already knew he'd been joking.

"I'd make a terrible personal chef," Payton said as she stood and started clearing the dishes. "Everyone would end up gaining ten pounds when all I did was feed them pie, my real passion."

"Pie?" Gigi and Alison said at the same time.

The pair looked at each other and laughed softly.

"Yes, I'm all about pie. I wish I had some here to share, but there are wedding cake samples in there if anyone wants dessert."

There was a rousing yes to the cake from everyone except Gigi.

"I'll get it," Atlas said.

While Payton cleared and loaded the dishwasher, Atlas plated and served the leftover cake from the tasting. But he didn't sit to eat his until she was ready to join him back at the table.

"What kind did I get?" Payton asked him when they were seated again.

"The mocha crunch. I've got the tiramisu," he said, eyeing his dessert. "I didn't know that flavor came in cake form until today."

"You're so sheltered," Payton teased. The truth was she'd never had that flavor in cake form either. But if she was going to eat tiramisu, she wanted the real thing. She was so adamant about it that she hadn't even bothered to try the sample before they picked the flavor of their wedding cake. Payton nudged Atlas's elbow. "Go on, give it a taste and tell us how it is."

"Glad to." He took a big bite, closed his eyes for dramatic effect, and nodded his approval. "It's—" Atlas's words were cut off, and his mouth opened and closed in a frantic motion as his lips instantly began to swell.

Someone screamed.

Someone else called out, "Atlas!"

"Payton, find his EpiPen. It should be in the kitchen somewhere. Probably the cupboard closest to the refrigerator," Gigi said calmly through the chaos.

She sprang into action, running into the kitchen to look for the medicine. She knew it was there. She'd seen it earlier. But where? She tried the cabinet closest to the fridge but didn't see it. Then she quickly started opening all the cabinets, knowing it was right in front. She hit paydirt on the third one. She snatched up the double pack and ran back to the table. By the time she got to his side, she already had the first pen out of the container and had removed the blue safety cap.

"It goes in the thigh, right?" she asked his family, making sure she was remembering correctly.

"Yes," Gigi said, worry radiating off her.

"Hurry," Alison pleaded. "I can't lose another brother."

The terror in Alison's voice was enough to almost break Payton. But when she looked down at Atlas's swollen lips and saw that he was starting to turn blue, she blocked everyone else out and jabbed him with the pen right through his jeans. After holding the pen there for fifteen seconds, she removed it and then grabbed Atlas's hand, holding on for dear life as his throat opened and he was able to breathe again.

Everyone was silent until finally Atlas croaked out, "Fire that pastry chef."

"Done," Alison said and ran over to give him a hug from the back. "You scared me, big bro."

"Scared me too," he said and pressed his hand to his throat.

"Atlas, we need to get you to a healer," Payton said, already rising from her chair.

"It's all right," he rasped.

"No, it isn't," she insisted. "We're going. Don't argue. Understand?"

He stared at her for a long moment and then rose from the chair, his legs shaky from the adrenaline.

"I've got you," Payton said, wrapping an arm around his waist. She glanced at his family, all of whom looked panic-stricken.

All of them except Gigi, who nodded firmly at Payton.

"Well done. I'll rest easy knowing Atlas has someone to look after him. Someone I can trust."

Payton swallowed the lump in her throat and nodded. She hated lying to her. But what else was she going to do? Tell her that this was all just part of the job? That she was being paid handsomely to pretend to be his wife? No, there was nothing to say. As much as she wanted to promise to always protect Atlas, that wasn't going to be her job after Sunday.

Her heart ached, and she wasn't sure if it was because of Atlas's ordeal or if she was already mourning the loss of him once their contract was over.

CHAPTER 20

"He'll live," Healer Harrison said as she ran her hands over Atlas's pulse points. "He'll need rest for the next twenty-four hours. While the effects of the shot wear off, he's going to feel like he got hit by a bus, but there's a potion I can send home with you that will help restore his energy."

"I've been through this before," Atlas said. His voice was full of fury, and rightly so. He'd been poisoned due to cross contamination by a careless chef.

Thoughts of lawsuits and negligence were swirling around in Payton's head, but she knew unless they could prove malice, there was no point. Besides, that was Atlas's call, not hers.

"Is it my imagination, or does it get worse each time this happens?" Atlas asked.

"It often does," the tall, blond-haired healer said with a

nod. "With each exposure, it can make the allergy worse. Do you know how you ingested coconut tonight?"

"It was a careless pastry chef," Payton answered for him. "I'm having his family throw out all the rest of the desserts so that this doesn't happen again."

"I'm sorry," the healer said. "The hardest part of this condition is that we can't control other people."

"But we can fire them," Payton said. "I'll just have to make the cake myself."

Atlas glanced at her, giving her a grateful smile.

Payton clutched his hand, the one she hadn't been able to let go of ever since they'd walked in. She knew he was going to be all right, but the events of the night had caught up to her, and she was starting to crash. Her stress response had left her exhausted. She couldn't even imagine how drained Atlas must feel.

"Take this," the healer said, handing Payton a potion bottle. She turned her attention back to Atlas. "It can sometimes make people nauseated, so drink it when you get home and then just take it easy until you're feeling like yourself again. If you get a good night's sleep, you'll probably feel better in the morning. Just don't run any marathons or put on a three-hour concert, okay?"

"No chance of that," he said.

"Good. Call me if you start to feel worse. Otherwise, just rest and have someone sanitize your kitchen."

"Already on it," Payton said.

The healer walked them out, and as they were heading to the rental car, she called, "Hey, Atlas?"

He paused and glanced back at her. "Yeah?"

"Loved the last album. Any chance I could get a photo for my niece?"

Payton winced. Poor guy. He'd almost died just an hour earlier, and now the healer wanted a photo. Seriously?

"Sure," he said, sounding slightly annoyed. But he pasted a smile on his face and allowed the selfie with Healer Harrison.

She gushed her gratitude, wished them happy holidays, and then rushed off.

"That was awkward," Payton said as they made their way to the car. "I can't believe she did that."

He let out a tired sigh. "Actually, I'm a little surprised it didn't happen sooner. People seem to lose all sense of boundaries around me. At least she waited to make sure I wasn't going to die before getting her social media proof."

Payton scowled. "I'm sorry. I really like Healer Harrison, but that was way over the line. I just can't believe people do stuff like that."

"That's nothing. Wait until I tell you about the dental hygienist who chipped my tooth on purpose just so I'd have to come back."

"They did not!" Payton exclaimed, completely outraged.

"They did. My lawyers threatened the practice with a massive lawsuit. In the end the hygienist was fired, and I was able to procure free dental work for my entire band and management company for as long as she's in business."

"That's..." She closed her eyes and took a deep breath, trying to collect herself. "I don't know how you do it, being in the spotlight like that."

"It's been a journey."

"Let's hope it's a quiet one for the rest of the evening."

EVERY INCH of Atlas's body ached as he crawled into bed. The achiness happened every time he'd had an anaphylactic shock episode, but this time it was all but unbearable. His body was still twitching with adrenaline, making him feel like he was going to come right out of his skin, and he was also in so much pain he could barely move. It was an awful state of being.

"Drink this," Payton said, handing him the potion the healer had prescribed.

His stomach turned just thinking about it, but he knew from experience it would help. "Thanks," he croaked out as he tried but failed to twist the cap off.

"Sorry. I should have done that," she said as she took it out of his hands. A few seconds later, she handed it back to him. "I'll go get you some water. Need anything else?"

"No." He took a long swig of the potion and grimaced. It tasted liked honey-flavored dirt with a hint of lavender.

"That bad?" she asked, wrinkling her nose.

"You have no idea." His stomach turned at the mere thought of drinking more of the distasteful concoction, but the sooner he got it down, the better he'd feel.

There was a light knock on the door followed by his sister calling, "Atlas? Can I come in?"

He made a face and shook his head. He did not want to see or talk to anyone. Not even Alison.

"I'll talk to her," Payton whispered and went to the door. A moment later, she slipped out and closed it behind her.

Atlas took another long drink of the potion and nearly gagged. As if the coconut hadn't been enough torture, now he had to endure this. The timing couldn't be worse when all he wanted to do was spend time with his grandmother. Earlier that day when they'd been playing cribbage, he'd just felt so... content. Like he was exactly where he was supposed to be.

His life outside of the cabin had faded away, and for a short time, he was just Alistair, the boy who'd grown up playing cards with his grandfather and dreaming of endless life possibilities. He liked feeling like that carefree kid again, even if only for fleeting moments. It made him feel human, like his life had value beyond what music he could unleash into the world. And that was something he didn't feel very often. Not these days.

The door opened and Payton slipped in, carrying a glass of water.

He gave her a weak smile. "Thanks for heading off my sister."

She placed the water on the nightstand and sat on the edge of the bed. "She just wanted to check on you and see if you needed anything. I told her you were already sleeping."

"You're brilliant." He downed the rest of the potion and made a face when his stomach protested.

"It's worse than I think, isn't it?" she asked, holding his hand and gently caressing the pad of his thumb.

"Way worse," he grumbled. "But it'll be worth it tomorrow when I'm not laid out flat in the bed all day."

"I hope so." She stood and headed toward the closet. "I'm going to grab some clothes and stay in another room tonight so that I don't disturb you while you sleep. If you need anything—"

"Don't," he said, cutting her off. "I'd rather you stayed here."

"That can't be true," she said gently. "You told me your body aches so much you feel like someone beat you up from the inside out. I just want you to heal tonight. Your family won't question anything. They know you're recovering. Wouldn't it be better for you to get a good night's sleep rather than trying to keep to our story?"

"It's not to keep up appearances," he said, sliding down into the covers. "I want you here." He reached out and gently tugged her back down on the bed. "I need you here."

She searched his gaze as if trying to read him. Finally she asked, "Are you sure? If you change your mind, let me know. I'll go sleep in one of the other rooms."

"I won't change my mind," he said as his heavy eyelids started to close.

"Okay, Atlas," she said softly and tried to get up again.

He tightened his grip, unwilling to let go. "Stay."

"I'm just going to get ready for bed. I'll be back soon." She leaned down and gave him a kiss on the corner of his mouth.

Atlas wanted to turn his head, to taste her lips, and to pull her down onto the bed with him, but he was just too weak. His head was filled with the image of her the night before, smiling and laughing in the horseless sleigh. The scenes shifted, each one flashing like a snapshot. Payton in the kitchen, Payton playing with the kittens, her head bent toward Gigi as she gave his grandmother her full attention, and finally, Payton wrapped around him as passion consumed them.

The bed shifted, pulling him out of his sleep haze. He opened his eyes to find Payton lying next to him, her hair fanned out on the pillow.

"You look like an angel," he said.

"So do you. A fallen one." She gave him the tiniest of smiles.

"Seems fitting." He rolled to his side and wrapped an arm around her waist, pulling her closer. As if she knew what he needed, she also rolled to her side, facing away from him so that he could spoon her from the back. He kissed the back of her neck and whispered, "Good night, angel."

"Good night, Atlas."

CHAPTER 21

"*How* long have you been making wedding cakes?" Gigi asked.

Payton looked up from where she was cutting the cake rounds so that they'd sit level on top of each other when she put them together. After a night of blissful sleep while being held by Atlas, she'd gotten up at the crack of dawn to get a jump on baking the cakes she'd need for their wedding cake the next day. Now that it was just after noon, the cakes were ready to be decorated.

Payton wiped her hands on a towel and then turned to give Gigi her full attention. "I just started this year, actually, when the inn started booking weddings. We had a woman in town who made wedding cakes, but she moved to Florida to be near her grandchildren, and there wasn't really anyone else that could do it last minute. So I stepped in and became the inn's official wedding cake gal. I haven't made that many of them. Maybe half a dozen."

"I bet with your magic, you make some pretty wonderful cakes," she said as she stroked St. Nick, the kitten. Payton had yet to see Gigi without that black and white kitten ever since she'd taken to him the day before.

"They're all right," Payton said, with a self-deprecating smile. "I'm not going to be winning any awards, but they taste good and photograph nicely."

"You're being modest," Gigi said.

Payton opened her mouth to protest, but when she looked into Gigi's curious eyes, she chose not to say anything. There was no point in trying to be modest. Gigi was seeing right through her. A swell of unease rose from deep in her gut. Did that mean that Gigi also knew about Atlas? She decided it was best not to ask.

Gigi chuckled softly to herself.

"What's funny?" Payton asked her.

"You. You want to argue, but you know I'm right."

"Ha. I guess so." Payton scrunched up her nose. "It just feels weird to boast about the stuff I make." She gave Gigi a wry smile. "Unless I'm trying to one-up my brother."

"Ah, sibling rivalry. I do miss my brother Petey when I see Alison and Alistair having a go at one another. It's a special relationship that only brothers and sisters can understand."

"True. Tell me about your brother," Payton said, giving Gigi her full attention.

"Oh, you want to know about Petey. What a light that one was." Pure joy lit her face, and Gigi seemed to just come to life. "He was the best. Protective, funny, earnest. He was the only person who could make me laugh when I was feeling blue. This one time…" She went on to describe numerous stories from their childhood. "But the best thing he ever did was introduce me to my Edgar. Do you want to know the funniest part about that?"

"Yes," Payton said, leaning forward and propping her chin up with her hand.

"I was actually seeing someone else at the time. Stewart Price. He was handsome, attentive, focused. He and Petey and Edgar were all friends. But Petey didn't think Stewart was right for me, so he interfered and made it so that Stewart stood me up. He sent Edgar in his place, and that was that. I knew within the hour that Edgar was for me. We were married three months later and spent over fifty years together before he passed."

"That seems kinda manipulative," Payton said. "I know it worked out in the end, but if my brother did that, he'd rue the day."

She snickered. "Don't think I didn't pay him back. Especially after I found out Stewart made partner at his firm at just twenty-eight years old. It was about then that I shredded all his underwear and cut holes in all his socks."

"You didn't." Payton couldn't stop laughing. Gigi was maybe the cutest grandmother she'd ever met.

"Oh, I did. Caused a big fight with Edgar too, since he didn't understand why I was so mad. We were married by then and couldn't have been happier. He said I should be thanking Petey. I guess he had a point, but it still wasn't my brother's place to interfere in my dating life like that. There were better ways to chop an onion."

"I take it Edgar didn't have a meddling brother?" Payton asked.

"Nope. He did have a sister though, so he was blinded by his biases. It's all right. Stewart ended up divorced three times, while Edgar and I—"

"Behaved like newlyweds up until the very end," Atlas said, appearing in the kitchen. His hair was tousled and his eyes still puffy with sleep, but he looked a thousand times better than he had the night before.

"You should only be so lucky," his grandmother told him with a sniff.

"From your lips to the goddess's ears, Gigi." He winked at her and headed toward the coffee pot.

Payton jumped up and hurried after him. She grabbed a mug and poured him a coffee. "I thought you might never get up today."

"I considered it. Might have even given in to that urge if you'd still been there when I woke up." He gratefully accepted the mug and took a sip.

"I had things to do."

He gave her a suggestive look that made her flush all the way to her toes.

"Stop flirting with me in front of Gigi," she said in a hushed whisper.

"Don't stop on my account," Gigi said, grinning at them. "I remember what it's like to be young and in love. Enjoy every moment of it."

"You heard her." Atlas leaned down, buried one hand in her hair, and then kissed her as if he were a starving man. By the time he let her go, she was breathless.

Payton stared up at him through unfocused eyes.

He just chuckled.

"Whoa." Gigi fanned herself with one hand.

"Yeah," Payton breathed.

"He comes by it honestly, you know. All of the men in the Frost family are very passionate. My Edgar had these moves that would leave me weak in the knees for days. And just between you and me, the size of his—"

"Okay, Gigi," Atlas said, cutting her off. "Payton doesn't need intimate knowledge of Grandpa's equipment."

"Is Gigi talking about Grandpa's nine inches again?" Danny asked as he walked into the dining room carrying Bells. The kitten was curled up against his chest, fast asleep.

"I wasn't going to say the actual size, but I thought Payton might like some tips on what to do with a man who's been blessed in that department. You know, so it's enjoyable for everyone."

Atlas choked on his coffee while Danny laughed.

"Oh, man," Danny said with a snort. "This is perfect. I love it when Gigi embarrasses the hell out of the edgy rock star. It sort of puts the world back in balance."

"I'm just keeping it real. Isn't that what the kids say?" Gigi asked Payton.

"Uh, sure?" Payton had no clue really. How could she keep up with the current generation's slang when she spent all her time in the kitchen?

"On that note, I'm going to go shower," Atlas said. "Maybe when I return, we can talk about something more respectable."

"Like what?" Gigi asked innocently. "Oh, I know. How

189

about you tell me all about that manscaping deal you signed earlier this year. In my day, we liked our men rugged. No need for fancy shavers that were 'perfect for your most intimate areas.' Did you try it out before you did that commercial, Alistair? Did you walk around hairless down there? What happened when it grew out? Wasn't it itchy? I have questions."

Danny was cracking up, laughing so hard that no sound was coming from his lips.

Meanwhile, Payton was just staring at her in admiration. Clearly, Gigi knew all about manscaping tools. She was just having the best time busting Atlas's balls.

"You think you're funny, don't you," Atlas said, shaking his head. "Go ahead, have your fun. I don't mind. But don't be surprised when you get your very own intimate shaving tool in your stocking, and then you can answer all your questions yourself." He gave her a pointed look and headed down the hall back toward the bedrooms.

Danny walked over and kissed Gigi on the check. "Have I told you how much I love you today?"

"Not yet," she said, beaming at him.

"I love you, Gigi. You're the absolute best."

"Love you, too, Danny." She handed him her kitten. "Can you take care of St. Nick for me? I'm afraid it's time for my afternoon nap."

"Sure, but don't you want help getting to your room?" he asked, frowning at her.

"I'll have Payton help me. I have something for her in my room."

Payton was full of admiration as she went to help the

older woman. They took it slow as they made their way down the hall with Gigi clutching Payton's arm. It was easy to forget how frail she was when they were all sitting around the cabin. Gigi was so warm and full of stories that it made Payton forget about her condition.

When they finally made it into Gigi's room and Payton got her situated on the bed, she said, "Gigi, I want to be just like you when I grow up."

Gigi patted her arm. "You're on your way already, gorgeous." She pointed to a small box on the dresser just across from the bed. "Can you get that for me?"

"Of course." Payton grabbed the small black box and handed it to Gigi.

Gigi patted the bed. "Have a seat, Payton."

"Okay." She sat with one leg folded on the bed and the other one hanging over the edge.

"This is for you." Gigi opened the box and pulled out a gorgeous antique ring that had a brilliant tourmaline that was the same color as Atlas's eyes. "It was my mother's, and the stone matched her eyes just like it does Alistair's. I thought it was only fitting that his wife have it. I trust you'll pass it on to the children you have. Or if you don't, then I just ask that when your time here on earth is done, that you pass it on to someone in the family."

Payton caught her breath and felt tears sting her eyes. She quickly blinked them back, but she was certain Gigi hadn't missed her sudden display of emotion. Her chest hurt as she forced out, "You are very kind, but I can't take this."

Gigi picked up the ring with her shaky hands and

carefully slipped it onto the ring finger of Payton's right hand. "Of course you can, Payton. Look, it's a perfect fit."

"It's not that. I..." What was she supposed to say? She couldn't exactly tell Gigi that she and Atlas weren't married and never would be. She supposed she should just take the ring and then immediately give it back to Atlas, but that seemed like more of a betrayal than pretending to get married. She wanted Gigi to give the ring to someone who deserved it, not the woman who was parading around lying to everyone. "This is truly lovely, Gigi," Payton said earnestly. "I just really think it should be given to someone in your immediate family. Like Alison, maybe."

"Alison already has some of my pieces. I've been saving this for the woman Alistair loves." She held Payton's hand between both of hers and stared at her with determination. "Not the woman he marries, Payton. The one he loves. His twin flame. The one who loves him unconditionally. That's you."

Payton hadn't missed a word she'd said. *Not the woman he marries. The one he loves.* Those words were pointed, carefully chosen. Payton cleared her throat. "I don't think I ever asked you what kind of witch you are."

She gave Payton a big smile. "I'm a spirit witch, just like Alistair."

"Which means what exactly?" Spirit witches had a wide range of strange abilities, and every spirit witch's ability was different.

"For starters, I'm a medium, also just like Alistair, though the spirits stopped visiting me about ten years ago. They prefer younger people because they feed off their energy. Mine isn't quite as attractive these days."

"They don't know what they're missing," Payton said.

"Thank you for that, but I'm not offended. Honestly, when I was younger I never noticed the energy drain. About twenty years ago, I really started to notice how much of a burden my gift was on me. It would leave me wiped out anywhere from a couple of hours to a couple of days. So I'm glad they've moved on."

"But that's not your only ability," Payton prodded.

Gigi gave her a noncommittal half nod.

"You're really going to make me work for it, aren't you?" Payton asked.

"You're not the only one with secrets, Payton. Let's just say that I've always known more than my grandson realizes. Tomorrow's event may not be everything that it seems, but mark my words, Payton McCabe, my grandson loves you. And it's clear you love him. I'm sure it's early days, but I'm never wrong. Take the ring. If for some reason down the road you think it should go to someone in the family, you choose who that might be. I'm leaving the decision with you. But I'll rest easy knowing that I gave it to the right person at the right time."

A single tear ran down Payton's cheek. She was so overwhelmed. It was clear that Gigi knew that she and Atlas weren't really married. And for some reason, she thought Payton and Atlas were end game and they'd marry eventually. So what had she done? She'd kept the news to herself and orchestrated a ceremony so that she could celebrate with them, even if it wasn't going to be a legal one.

"I'd appreciate it if you'd keep what I just said to yourself," Gigi added. "I know my grandson. It's better if he comes around to the truth on his own."

Payton sucked in a sharp breath and tried her best to get her emotions under control. "You Frosts sure do like your secrets, don't you?"

"Glass houses, Payton," she said, patting her hand. "You had your reasons for agreeing to this. Alistair and I have ours."

What could she say to that? Nothing. Gigi was right.

"Now go on and finish that cake. We have a wedding to attend tomorrow."

Payton stood and couldn't help glancing down at the ring on her finger. "What should I tell Atlas about this?"

"The truth. That I wanted you to have it." She settled her head on her pillow. "Tell one of the boys to get me before dinner."

"I will." Dismissed, Payton left and closed the door softly behind her. She stood there for a long moment, wondering what she should do. Put the ring away or just wear it? Her head was telling her to go tuck it safely away in the bedroom she was sharing with Atlas, but her heart screamed for her to wear it. It would make Gigi happy. And no one would question it except Atlas. Did she want to have that conversation with him? No. But she didn't want to take the ring off either. Gigi had touched her heart, and Payton wanted to honor that.

Decided, Payton headed for the kitchen, ready to decorate her own wedding cake.

CHAPTER 22

"*A* toast to the happy couple!" Alison said as she raised her wine glass.

Everyone except Atlas raised a similar glass of wine. After his ordeal the day before, he'd decided to stick with water until he was sure he was running on all cylinders again.

"To the happy couple!" they all echoed.

Payton took a sip of her wine and then put it aside. Her nerves were shot. If she felt this anxious the night before her fake wedding, what was she going to feel like when it was the real deal? She pushed the thought aside and tried not to think about it.

It wasn't long before Gigi said her goodnights and had Alison help her to bed.

As they were leaving, Patty took a seat by Payton. "Can I help you with anything? You look like you might be ready to vomit. Antacid? A gummy? The ones I have put you right to sleep. Or maybe a getaway car?" She glanced over at Atlas. "I know he's gorgeous, but no one would blame you if you couldn't handle a rock star's lifestyle."

Payton gaped at Atlas's aunt. Was she really offering to help Payton escape the night before her wedding when Payton hadn't said anything about having second thoughts? So much for Frost family loyalty. "I'm okay. I think I'm just going to turn in soon. But first I have to talk to Olivia and find out if she's heard anything about my dress. It was supposed to arrive today from Washington."

Patty winced. "Ouch. But I heard you have a backup, so that's good, right? Excellent planning, really, considering how last minute this whole thing turned out to be."

"Yeah, it's a good thing," Payton said and got to her feet. She collected the empty wine glasses and headed to the kitchen. After cleaning up, she said goodnight to Danny, Tim, and Atlas.

"I'll be right behind you," Atlas said and was met with wolf whistles and cheering from his cousin and uncle.

"Cute," Payton said dryly as she shook her head and went to go find Alison.

Just before she reached Gigi's room, Alison slipped out and leaned against the door as she let out a long sigh.

"Everything okay?" Payton asked, her heart racing. Was Gigi all right? She'd seemed a little tired after dinner, but otherwise she'd been in good spirits.

"Yeah," Alison said, sounding exhausted. "It's just hard, you know? Just last year she was still driving, and now... I have to be on guard when she's in the shower in case she needs anything, help her get dressed, help her get anywhere around the house. And before you ask, no, she won't use a wheelchair. She says the moment she gets one of those will be the moment she'll lose all mobility. And you know what, Payton?"

"What?" she asked, sensing that Alison was just stressed and nursing a broken a heart. She just needed to vent; she didn't need solutions.

"She's right. The fact that she does her best to move around as much as she can is probably the reason she's still with us. I'm grateful. It's just hitting me hard after seeing her so tired tonight."

Payton forgot about all her worries and tugged Alison into a hug. "She loves you and appreciates everything you've done this weekend. You know that, right?"

Alison nodded even as a sob got caught in her throat. "I'm just…"

"Stressed. Anyone would be," Payton soothed, wondering if Alison had anyone in her life that watched over her. She'd been the driving force behind getting the wedding put together and had done a fantastic job. But now? She needed someone to lean on.

"Come on. Let's get you to your room." Payton wrapped her arm around Alison's waist and guided her to the room she was using. "I'm going to draw you a bath and then get you some tea. It's time for you to relax. You've done everything you can. Tomorrow will be wonderful, and we have you to thank for it."

"Except your dress isn't here," she said with a sniff. "I was on the phone for forty-five minutes with the shipping company, and they swear it's still coming. But with the snow coming down, I doubt it." She hugged Payton tighter. "I'm sorry. I know you loved it."

Disappointment washed over Payton, but she ignored it. "It's just a dress. The backup will be fine." As she said the words, the disappointment seemed to soak right into her bones. She tried to shake the feeling, but it had taken hold and wasn't letting go.

Get a grip, Payton, she silently berated herself. *It's just a dress.*

She knew the dress meant nothing, so why was she so disappointed?

Alison let go and wiped at her eyes. "I'm sorry. I guess I just needed a moment to get myself together. I'll be fine."

"Of course you will," Payton reassured her. "But right now, you're going to let me take care of you."

Alison's lips twitched up into the tiniest hint of a smile.

After running a bath in the oversized tub and adding a soothing bath bomb, Payton found a thick robe and handed it to her. "Get in the bath. I'll be right back with tea."

"It's kind of nice having a sister," Alison said and then disappeared into the bathroom.

Payton couldn't help but agree.

When she returned with the chamomile tea, she found Alison in the tub reading a paperback book. "Perfect," she said, handing Alison the mug.

"This was exactly what I needed, Payton. Thank you."

"No problem. Now don't worry about a thing. Not even the dress. Just relax and get some sleep. Tomorrow we'll celebrate."

"Yes, we will."

"THERE YOU ARE," Atlas said when Payton walked into their room. He gave her a cheeky grin. "Did you get lost?"

"Actually, I was giving Alison a pep talk," she said as she grabbed her pajamas from the dresser. "Are you done with the bathroom?"

"Yep," he said, leaning against the headboard, leaving his delicious abs exposed.

Payton waited to lick her lips until she was safely in the bathroom with the door closed. Despite being tired and disappointed about her dress, she was still wildly attracted to the man in the other room. It didn't help that Gigi had called her out, insisting that Payton was in love with him. How could that be true? She'd only known him for less than a week. Could someone fall in love that quickly?

Gigi said she had. She'd known the first time she met Edgar, and by Gigi's account, they'd had a wonderful life together.

Not that Payton expected Atlas to marry her or even reciprocate her feelings. He was a rock star after all. It didn't matter that he'd proved himself to be thoughtful and caring and a hell of a lot of fun. When his time in Christmas Grove was over, he'd leave and Payton wouldn't be going with him.

As she got ready for bed, she briefly wondered if she'd even consider living a life that had her traveling all over the world, staying in hotel after hotel after hotel.

No. Not just no, but hell no. The very idea was panic inducing.

Payton didn't just crave a simple life in Christmas Grove,

she thrived on it. She knew herself well enough to know that if she decided to follow Atlas, she'd go into it with the best of intensions. But eventually that kind of life would break her. She needed roots.

It was ingrained in her DNA.

Her heart felt heavy. How was it fair to find someone like Atlas, only to have him for a very short time?

She stared in the mirror at her reflection and made a snap decision. If she only had tonight and tomorrow, she was going to make memories that would be forever burned into her brain.

It was just too bad that she hadn't brought anything other than her cotton pajamas that covered practically every inch of her body. A little satin or lace would go a long way to set the mood. With no other options, she undid the top two buttons of her pajama top and mussed her hair to give it a little bit of volume.

She checked her reflection one last time, decided she'd looked worse, and then walked back into the bedroom to find Atlas was already asleep.

"Son of a melting snowman," she muttered before turning out the lights and climbing into her side of the bed. She rolled over onto her side and waited a few beats to see if Atlas would wrap his arm around her and spoon her like he had the night before, but when all he did was let out a tiny snore, she sighed and resigned herself to sleep.

CHAPTER 23

*a*tlas woke to a bright room filled with sunshine. The light was streaming through the window and casting plenty of sparkles on the fresh layer of snow outside. He smiled to himself, pleased that today of all days was filled with light.

He rolled over and propped himself up on one elbow so that he could admire the beauty who was still sleeping next to him. He hadn't meant to fall asleep before she even came to bed the night before, but he'd been no match for the exhaustion that had gripped him after the coconut incident. And although the healer had been correct about the potion helping by morning, it hadn't done much to improve his energy level. He knew from experience the only solution to that was to get a good night's sleep.

"Hey, you," Payton said, blinking her sleep-filled eyes. "How are you feeling?"

"Great. Happy wedding day," he said with a wink.

Payton groaned. "Don't remind me."

His good mood instantly soured, and he frowned.

"Stop," she said with a soft smile as she reached up to soothe his wrinkled brow. "I was just thinking about how the weekend was going to end today, and then I'll have to go back to the real world. I was getting used to playing with kittens and hearing all your grandmother's stories about baby Alistair."

"Is that it? And here I was thinking that you'd rather be doing anything other than marrying me." He hadn't meant to voice his insecurities, but there they were, and there was no taking them back now.

"Not true at all. Who wouldn't want to marry the gorgeous and talented Atlas Mazer?" she teased.

Payton McCabe. He kept the thought to himself and instead focused on the sexy woman in his bed. "You look gorgeous with the morning light kissing your skin."

Her lips curved into a slow smile. "You're flirting awfully early in the morning, aren't you?"

"I can't help it," he said as he reached out and ran a finger along her exposed shoulder and down her chest until he brushed the swell of her breast.

Payton, who was holding his gaze, sucked in a sharp breath as she arched into his touch.

The chemistry between them crackled, and Atlas thought he'd die if he didn't get to touch her everywhere. "Do you mind if I do this?" he asked as he released another of her buttons.

She gave him a tiny shake of her head as she licked her lips.

It was all he needed to know. He made quick work of her sleep shirt and then covered her body with his as he took her mouth, claiming her, making her his in the only way that he could.

Sometime later, when Payton's sated and pliable body was tucked close to his, he brushed a lock of hair out of her eyes and pressed a tender kiss to her swollen lips. When he pulled away, he said, "That was incredible."

"Yeah," she breathed, her blue eyes brighter than he'd ever seen them.

He pulled her closer and rolled onto his back so that she was partially lying on top of him. Atlas hadn't ever been one for cuddling after sex, but he wanted nothing more than to feel her bare skin pressed against his as he slowly caressed her smooth back with his fingers.

The passion had ignited like a flame between them, and Atlas wondered if he'd ever wanted anyone the way he'd craved Payton. The answer was a resounding no, and he knew in that moment that no matter how much he wanted to lie to himself, he wasn't ever going to be able to let her go.

Smiling down at her, he said, "That was one hell of a way to start our wedding day."

She let out a nervous chuckle and nodded. Then before he could say anything else, she started to pull out of his arms and said, "Speaking of the wedding, I better get up and—"

"What's that?" he asked when his gaze landed on the antique ring she was wearing. He reached out and caught her right hand in his, moving her hand so that he could inspect the familiar ring closer.

"It's exactly what you think it is," she said softly. "Gigi gave it to me yesterday."

He blinked down at her and spoke before he could rein his words back in. "That's a family heirloom." The words hung in the air between them, and they both understood the implication of his statement.

"I know, Atlas. I told her I couldn't take it and that she should give it to someone in the family, but she insisted. She told me that the ring was always meant for the woman who loves her grandson, Alistair Frost, and that's who she was giving it to." Payton rolled out of his arms and sat up, pulling her sleep shirt back on, much to his disappointment.

"Of course she said that. She thinks we're married," he said, sitting up with her.

Payton pressed her lips together in a thin line, and he got the feeling she wanted to say something else, but she didn't. Instead, she slipped out of bed and headed for the bathroom. She paused and looked back at him. "I'm wearing it because she wants me too. If and when that changes, I promise I won't run off with your family heirloom. Okay?"

"Of course. Payton, I never meant to imply that you'd do that," he said quickly, feeling like a complete jackass. He hadn't meant to make her feel as if she were stepping out of line by wearing the ring, he'd just been caught off guard. He hadn't expected Gigi to give Payton such a meaningful gift.

Though if he was honest, he liked that the ring that had always been meant for his wife was on her hand. He didn't want her to take it off. So why had he wigged out?

She gave him a short nod and disappeared into the bathroom.

~

"You look... rested," Alison said as she sipped from a coffee mug.

"I am rested," Atlas agreed as he grabbed a mug from the cabinet and couldn't help smiling.

Alison chuckled. "You've found yourself a good one, big brother." She patted his arm as she moved past him. "Don't eff it up."

His smile vanished because Atlas knew that he very much was on the verge of doing just that. Everything between him and Payton that morning had been electric. It was a connection that was unlike any other. And if he'd had his way, he'd still be back in that bed with her, loving every inch of her until they were both too spent to even move. And then he'd do it again, and again, and again, every night until she got sick of him.

But he'd ruined it when he'd freaked out about that damned ring.

He set his mug down and marched back down the hall to their bedroom.

"Payton!" he called as he strode in, looking for her.

The bathroom door swung open, and she appeared

wearing a robe and a towel wrapped around her head. "What is it? Is Gigi okay?"

"No, I mean, yes, Gigi is fine. I just... I think I owe you an apology."

Her body relaxed as she leaned against the doorframe. "Yeah, you probably do."

He couldn't help it, he chuckled. "You know, that's one of the things I love about you."

She raised both eyebrows. "What? That I call you out on your shit?"

"Yes." He walked over to her, grabbed the belt of her robe, and tugged her to him. "You don't treat me like a rock star. I like that. Maybe a little too much."

Her eyes danced with humor. "Are you saying you like me?"

"I wouldn't be marrying you today if I didn't like you," he quipped.

The humor faded from her eyes, and he once again felt like he'd messed up somehow.

"Payton," he said, frowning at her. "Are you having second thoughts? If you don't want to do this then—"

"It's not that," she said quickly and then let out a long breath. "I have a confession to make."

"Don't tell me you're already married. That'd be a little awkward," he teased, trying to lighten the moment. Whatever she had to say, she seemed nervous, and he just wanted to put her at ease.

She rewarded him with a laugh. "Hardly. Here's the thing; I think I like you too much."

"And that's a problem, why?"

"Because, Atlas, later today I'm going to walk down that aisle, pledge to love you for the rest of my days, and seal it with a kiss. And then by the time the holidays are over, you're going to be gone and out of my life. It's going to hurt, no matter what. And while it was wonderful and I don't regret it for one second, after what we shared this morning, I know I'm not going to get out of this unscathed. That's why I bristled when you implied that I shouldn't be wearing your great-grandmother's ring. You should know me better than to think that I'd run off with the family jewels. If you don't, then—"

"I do trust you," he insisted. "I was just caught off guard, and not for the reason you think. I never thought you'd run off with that ring. That's not you. Anyone who's known you for ten minutes could see that."

"Then why?" She frowned up at him. "What was it that got you so spooked?"

"Isn't it obvious?" he asked, searching her eyes.

"You thought she was going to find out this is all a sham?"

"No, Payton." He shook his head, exasperated. "She won't find that out, because it's not a sham. At least not completely. Don't you get it? I'm falling for you, too, only I didn't know it until I saw that ring. And then I freaked out."

"You're falling for me?" she asked, looking dumbfounded.

"Yes."

"You're sure?"

"Yes," he said again. And this time, he sealed it with a

kiss. When they broke apart, he pressed his forehead to hers and asked, "Does that clear things up?"

"No, not really," she said, laughing. "But I'm no longer mad at you, so that's something."

He chuckled. "See you at the altar this afternoon?"

She nodded. "I'll be there with bells on."

CHAPTER 24

$\mathcal{P}$ ayton stared at herself in the mirror and tried not to scowl. There was no denying that her long blond hair looked better than it ever had. She didn't know what Alison had done to it, but Atlas's sister was a genius. For the first time in her life, her hair was shiny and smooth with big soft waves, making her look like a million bucks.

Olivia had been just as brilliant when it came to her makeup. Since Payton spent all her days in the kitchen, she never bothered to learn how to put on what she called a 'fancy face.' On any given day, Payton wore sunscreen, lip balm, and maybe the tiniest bit of mascara. Today, she had a gorgeous smoky eye, highlighter above her rosy cheeks, and a deep red lip that made her look like high glamour.

The only problem was the dress.

The one they'd had overnighted had never arrived, leaving her stuck with her second choice. She knew being upset about it was childish. One day when she got married for real, she could wear the other one. Or something like it. But she doubted it. From now on, she'd always associate that dress with Atlas, and that wouldn't bode well for whoever her future groom might be.

"You look amazing," Olivia said. "Truly, a bride fit for a magazine cover."

"If you say so," Payton said with a put-upon sigh. "I just can't help but feel something's off. I just wish—"

"Payton! Oh my gosh, you're not going to believe this," Alison said as she rushed in the bridal suite. "Look at what just showed up via private messenger."

Payton turned and spotted a giant cardboard box that was taller than her. Alison had put it on a small roller cart. Payton briefly wondered where she'd found that handy accessory and then dismissed the thought. This was Alison she was talking about. The woman was a miracle worker when it came to organizing things. "I'm afraid to get my hopes up. After the trouble we've had this weekend finding the right dress, I'm fully expecting it to be one of Blake's cupcake gowns. Or worse, one that makes me look like I'm auditioning to be a stripper at the Brides and Rhinestones cowboy bar."

"Where's that?" Alison laughed. "Sounds like a ton of fun."

Payton waved an impatient hand. "San Francisco. But never mind that. Let's get this box open."

The three of them dismantled the box in no time and found Payton's perfect dress hanging inside. It even looked like Noel's employees had steamed it before they'd sent it.

"Oh, wow," Payton said in a reverent tone. "It's my dress."

"It sure is." Alison clapped her hands together. "Let's hurry up and get you in it before you miss your own wedding."

Olivia scoffed. "They can't start without the bride."

"True," Payton said. "But I don't want Gigi waiting outside longer than she has to."

Alison gave her a grateful smile, and then they got to work on switching gowns.

ATLAS COULDN'T STOP FIDGETING. He was standing under an arbor out near the lake as the sun sparkled off the fresh white snow. The few seats they'd set up were filled with his family and Payton's brother. Every one of them stared at Atlas, and he guessed they were all wondering if he had a runaway bride.

He had to admit he was wondering, too. How long did it take to get into a wedding dress? Over thirty minutes, it seemed. Atlas had glanced at his watch more times in the last five minutes than he had in the last five months. What was taking Payton so long? And why was he so worried?

His nerves were getting the best of him, and he didn't know what to do about it.

It's not real, he told himself over and over and over again. But each time he insisted the wedding was a sham, he heard a resounding *no* as the universe pushed back.

"Relax, man," Danny whispered. "She'll be here. She married you once already, right?"

Atlas looked at his best man and just nodded. He wished he could relax, but his nerves were in overdrive, and he was fairly certain that the only thing that would calm him down was if Payton was standing right in front of him ready to say *I do.*

Goddess above, he was losing it.

Just when he thought he'd come right out of his skin if he had to wait any longer, the wedding music started and Olivia appeared in a simple red dress with white ankle boots. She was holding a bouquet of white daisies with a couple of the red sunflowers that would match Payton's.

It seemed to take three years for Olivia to make it to the arbor and then another three for Payton to appear. But when she did, she took his breath away. Atlas was certain he'd never seen a woman more beautiful than the one walking toward him. Her face was flushed, and her hair looked like spun gold. When he took in the dress she was wearing, she was so lovely that all he could think about was getting her out of it.

Payton met his gaze and gave him one of her slow, shy smiles, and he felt his heart melt right there. This woman was going to kill him. He loved everything about her and prayed that by the end of this they'd somehow find a way to stay together. Because no way could he picture himself walking away from Payton McCabe.

The moment that Payton stopped in front of Atlas and placed her hands in his, all of his racing thoughts vanished. He met her gaze, smiled, and felt at peace for the first time in months. It was weird how that happened to him. It seemed that through his entire music career, all the stress came with the anticipation of an event or performance. But when it came time to play or sit for interviews, he was strangely calm and focused.

Just like he was now when the officiant asked him to repeat his vows. He did as he was asked, lingering on the section that promised to love and honor the other person for better or worse. That's what he wanted. Someone he could be himself around and who would love him for *him*, not his accolades and the size of his bank account. And his someone was clearly Payton.

When the officiant asked Payton to repeat her vows, tears suddenly filled her eyes. She laughed through the tears but didn't bother to try to hold them back as she repeated her vows.

"By the power vested in me by the state of California, I now pronounce you married," the officiant said. "You may kiss each other."

Payton let out a little *whoop* the moment Atlas wrapped his arms around her. He dipped her backward and sealed the deal with a mind-numbing scorcher of a kiss. Somewhere in the back of his mind, he heard their families clapping and hollering their approval, but all he was interested in was her. The one who'd just promised to love him forever. And if he had his way, he was going to hold her to it.

When he finally placed her back on her feet, she was breathless when she said, "Looks like we did it."

He grinned. "We definitely did."

CHAPTER 25

*P*ayton stood at the floor-to-ceiling windows in the great room of the cabin and did her best to take in every last magical detail. The dancing snow people, the animated gnomes and elves, the miniature angels that lived in the live Christmas trees. She was going to miss this place. Not just the cabin and the magic that had been spun there this weekend, but also the people she'd shared it all with.

Olivia and Declan had left a few hours after the ceremony. Not long after that, Aunt Patty, Uncle Tim, and Cousin Danny had all said their goodbyes, citing weather and traffic and work obligations as to why they had to get going. Danny had taken Bells and promised to take good care of the mischievous kitten. That left only St. Nick, who was currently glued to Gigi's side.

"I'm all packed," Alison said from behind her.

Payton turned around to find her wedding fairy all

bundled up in a red coat and matching scarf. She too had to take off for home so she could go into work the next day. Monday morning was coming awfully fast, and there wasn't anyone else available to open her craft gallery. With it being Christmas season, she couldn't afford for it to be shut down for even one day if she wanted to meet her year-end goals.

"I'm going to miss you," Payton said, giving her faux sister-in-law a giant hug. "You better stay in touch."

"I will. You can count on that," she said, her voice muffled.

"And make sure and let me know if you have any of Danny's pottery mugs in stock. That would be the perfect gift for Olivia and Declan," Payton added when they broke apart.

"You got it." Alison looked Payton up and down and raised one eyebrow. "Are you going to wear that dress forever? I would've thought you'd have changed out of it by now."

Payton smoothed her hands down the wedding dress that she loved so much and felt her face flush. "I only get to wear it for one day. I might as well enjoy it, right?"

"Or you just want to wait for my smelly brother to take it off you," she said with a wrinkle of her nose. "I mean, I suppose that's what newly married people do, but gross."

Payton laughed. "There's that, too. Plus, I didn't really have anything else to wear for our little reception, so this is it. Make fun of me if you will, but I'm choosing joy today."

"As you should." Alison gave her one last hug and whispered, "Take care of Gigi for me. Don't let Atlas sneak her too many cookies. They give her heartburn."

"Do you really think I'm going to deprive her of any treat she wants?" Payton asked incredulously. The woman was on her last days. "If she wants to eat all the cookies, I'll gladly supply her with antacids."

Alison rolled her eyes. "You and my brother are just alike. I guess it really was a match made in the mystic."

"I'm just saying she deserves whatever indulgence she wants. She's earned it," Payton said with a shrug.

"You're not wrong. I just don't want her to be uncomfortable." Alison grabbed her bag and said, "Tell Atlas he needs to return the other dress by the end of the week. I don't want him to forget. Okay?"

"On it," Payton said and walked Alison to the door. "Did you already say goodbye to Atlas and Gigi?"

Alison's eyes misted with tears as she nodded. "I did. It's hard leaving after a trip like this. Our family isn't very big, but we're all spread out in different towns. I always forget how much I love spending time with them."

"You're lucky to have them." Payton had always wanted a family like theirs. Instead, she'd gotten dysfunctional parents who could barely handle themselves, much less two kids. At least she had Declan. And now Olivia. And she was grateful for them both.

"I know. Okay, I'm out."

Payton waved as her new friend climbed into her vehicle and then took off down the long driveway. She was just shutting the door when Atlas came up behind her.

"Hey, gorgeous. Are you ready to get out of that dress?" he asked.

"Only if you're the one taking it off me."

"I'm not going to say no to that." In one swift motion, he leaned down and lifted her up, sweeping her off her feet.

Payton let out a *whoop* of surprise and then wrapped her arms around his neck and snuggled against his well-defined chest as he carried her to their room.

When he put her back down on her feet, she gazed up at him and couldn't stop herself from asking, "Atlas?"

"Yeah?" he said as he bent down and nuzzled her neck.

"What happens next?"

He lifted his head and met her gaze, humor lighting his eyes. "Do you mean as in a step by step of what I'm going to do to you now? Because if you want a play-by-play, I'm happy to both explain and demonstrate. Like right now, I can see your pulse beating right here." He ran a light thumb over her neck. "And I can't help but want to taste it." He moved in to do just that, but Payton took a step back.

She put a hand up in front of her, more as a self-control move than anything else. Good goddess, there was no question that she was weak around this man. "That's quite... lovely," she said, her voice a little husky.

"Lovely, huh? Then why did you stop me?"

She cleared her throat. "Because I meant what happens next between you and me. I'm not trying to pressure you; I could just use a clear picture so that we're on the same page."

All the playfulness from her faux groom vanished. "You mean what happens when I go back on tour?"

"Yes and no. I mean, like right now, what are we? Together? Dating? Exclusive? Nonexclusive? Just hooking up?"

"We are *not* just hooking up," he said, sounding offended. "And I thought we covered this before the ceremony. That we're together and definitely exclusive."

She placed a hand on his chest right over his heart and smiled up at him. "There's no need to get worked up. I was just asking the question. Communication is a good thing."

"Yeah, okay," he said, still sounding annoyed. But his chest wasn't puffed up anymore, and some of the tension had melted from his shoulders. "As far as when I go back on the road, we'll just have to work it out. You can come visit me on the days that work for you, and I can come back to Christmas Grove during my breaks. While I'm traveling, we can do FaceTime."

"That's reasonable," she said, except she knew she sounded skeptical.

"What is it, Pay? Is there a problem with the plan?" he asked.

"No. There's absolutely nothing wrong with it. It's just that I don't get many days off, and with travel schedules, I'm not sure how it's going to work for me to come see you." She bit down on her bottom lip, looking stressed.

"Do you get two days off in a row?" he asked.

"Yes."

"Then that's all we need. I'll send a private jet to get you, and we'll meet up wherever I am. When it's time to go back, the jet will take you home. I'm sure there's a regional airport around here somewhere, so you won't even need to worry about getting to the Sacramento airport."

"Private jet? I couldn't do that. It's too much," she protested.

"It's not too much," he insisted. "If I want to see you, it's the easiest way to make it happen. Don't punish both of us just because you don't want to appear to be using me. Trust me, you won't be. And if it ever becomes a problem, I'll tell you. All right?"

Payton still felt weird about the entire thing, but she was in no position to fight him on it. He was right. If they wanted to spend any time together, she'd have to get over her fear of taking advantage of his wealth. She never wanted to be that person. She reached up and caressed his jawline and then smiled. "All right."

"All right?" he asked again, this time with excitement in his tone.

"Yes, Atlas. I won't turn down a ride in your private jet if it means I get to spend time with you," she confirmed.

"Thank the gods. Now, can I get you out of this dress?" he asked, already reaching for the zipper on the back.

She chuckled softly. "Yes, please. I've been waiting all day for you to do just that."

Payton turned around and lifted her hair, giving him better access.

Atlas placed both hands on her hips, and instead of dealing with the zipper, he ran his tongue along the nape of her neck and then placed soft kisses all along her spine, making her shiver with anticipation. The one thing she'd learned during their night together was that Atlas Mazer liked to take his time. And she was here for it.

"I never knew what I was missing," he murmured as he finally started to unzip her dress. "If I'd known last New Year's Eve what I know now, there's no way I'd have kept my distance. Just think of all the fun we could have been having this year if we'd only known that this thing we have is so explosive."

Every inch of Payton's body was vibrating with anticipation. She wanted him to take his time, yet she was desperate for him to get down to business. "Atlas, please," she breathed.

"Please, what?" he asked. But before she could answer, he cocked his head to the side and added, "Do you hear that?"

"Hear what?" All she could hear was the blood rushing in her ears.

"That. It sounds like scratching."

Payton turned her attention to where he was listening, and that's when she heard the tiny little *meow*. "It's St. Nick." She quickly stepped out of her wedding dress, grabbed a nearby robe, and ran to the door. She jerked it open and found the black and white kitten sitting there staring up at her.

"Meow."

"What are you doing out here, sweetie pie?" she asked the kitten as she turned around to face Atlas. "Wasn't she in Gigi's room when you left them tonight?"

He nodded slowly and then suddenly took off running.

Payton clutched the kitten to her chest and followed Atlas to Gigi's room. When she got there, her heart damn near burst into a million little pieces when she saw Atlas holding his grandmother's lifeless body.

CHAPTER 26

*I*t's time to go, Atlas, Ashton said for what seemed like the hundredth time. *There's work to be done.*

Atlas scowled at his brother and went back to dealing with his grandmother's estate paperwork. It had been a week since she'd passed. An entire week of living on this earth without his favorite person. If it hadn't been for Payton, he didn't know how he'd have survived it. "I can't go until this is done," Atlas insisted.

Bullshit. That's what you pay people for.

"Why are you in such a hurry to leave Christmas Grove?" Atlas demanded. "I don't have any shows lined up until January. There's nothing to go back to."

That's not true. You have a bunch of shows the week before Christmas.

"What?" Atlas frowned. "I canceled those so I could spend December with Gigi."

You tried to cancel them, but the label said no. Check your website. They're still listed, and all the shows are sold out.

Atlas quickly grabbed his laptop and let out a string of curses before he called his manager. Twenty minutes later, after many threats from both sides, Atlas ended the call and slumped into a chair, holding his head in his hands.

Sure enough, Ashton had been correct. They hadn't canceled that run of shows and cited something in the contract about only canceling for specific reasons. Spending time with a dying grandmother wasn't one of them. When he said he was grieving because his beloved grandmother had actually died, they said his contract only allowed a bereavement period of ten days. In short, unless he wanted to get sued by his label and all the venues, he was going to have to head back out on the road a lot sooner than he'd planned.

He buried his fingers in his hair that had gotten too long and pulled as hard as he could while he let out a loud stream of expletives.

Feel better?

"No!" he barked at his brother and then got up to pace the too-large cabin. He was still at the lake house in Christmas Grove and had planned to stay there until New Year's Day. If he'd had his way, he'd stay even longer. While he'd known his time with his grandmother was coming to an end, he hadn't been prepared for just how hard he'd take her loss. For most people, a world without Gigi in it was just a little less bright. But for him, it was like he'd been plunged into darkness, and the only one who seemed to help him see the light of day was Payton.

I have a song I've been working on, Ashton said.

Atlas closed his eyes and took a deep breath. Hitting his brother was useless, but if he ignored him, that would get under his skin. Instead of replying to his brother, he picked up his phone again and called the family lawyer who was helping him deal with his grandmother's estate.

"Jenson? It's Atlas. I'm going to need to hand everything over to you. It looks like I have some bookings I can't get out of and—"

"Say no more," the lawyer said. "Send me all the paperwork, and I'll get a dedicated staffer working on it. We'll only call you when we need a decision or a signature."

"Thanks." He ended the call and felt even worse. Dealing with the estate was his last connection to Gigi. Letting it go was rough.

With nothing else to do but wait for Payton to get back, Atlas headed to the bar area that was just off the kitchen and made himself a stiff drink. Despite the reputation being a musician usually implied, he really wasn't a big drinker. He usually only had one or two drinks in social settings and almost never drank when he was alone.

This was the exception. Or at least it was close enough. Because Atlas wasn't actually alone. Ashton was there, and he wouldn't stop badgering him to get his next song down on paper.

"Ashton, if you don't leave me alone, I'm going to sage your ass right out of here," Atlas threatened.

You've been saying that for at least ten years. I'm not worried.

"You should be," Atlas grumbled.

Get out your pen. You need a distraction.

"If I do this, will you leave me alone for the next twelve hours at least? I would like some alone time with my girlfriend, and you being around is a real mind-bender."

Fine. Ashton crossed his arms over his chest and waited.

Begrudgingly, Atlas went to find his notebook and pen. Then he took a seat and waited. He'd just get this song down and then get busy packing.

Only as soon as Ashton started singing the words to his new song, Atlas's heart nearly burst right out of his chest. The imagery, the haunting sadness, the callbacks to a happy childhood.

The song was about love and loss and about living in a void where no one ever moves forward. When he sang the final word, *hopeless,* Atlas knew it was Ashton's story, and for the second time that week, he just felt broken.

"I CAN'T BELIEVE they're making you work right after losing Gigi," Payton said, fire flashing in her eyes as she ranted about Atlas's label, his management, and the venues, none of which had even acknowledged Atlas's loss.

"I know." Atlas reached out and pulled her into a hug. They were standing on the tarmac of the local regional airport. "They're shits for making me do this."

"Yeah, they are," she said with a sad chuckle. "I just can't believe you're leaving so soon. I was really getting used to having you around."

They'd spent the last ten days together at the cabin, taking walks and playing with St. Nick while Payton

A WITCH FOR MR. FROST

listened to all of Atlas's favorite memories that included Gigi. It had been both painful and cathartic. Now he was leaving, and he felt like his heart was being ripped out of his chest. "I'll be back before you know it."

"New Year's?" she asked, frowning.

"New Year's Day," he confirmed, hating that they'd be apart for Christmas, but it couldn't be helped. He had a show on both Christmas Eve and the day after Christmas, both of them on the East Coast.

"All right. I knew what I was signing up for when I started dating a rock star."

"Married," he teased.

She held up her left hand to prove it. Ten days after their fake wedding, and she was still wearing his ring, and neither of them had said anything about taking it off.

He grabbed both her hands, ran his thumb over the antique ring Gigi had given her, and then kissed her softly on the lips. They both knew that the tourmaline ring was more important to him, so it wasn't a surprise to her that he always touched it as if reminding himself of Gigi.

"Do you have your compass?" she asked.

"Right here." He pulled it out of his pocket and suppressed the sigh that always overtook him when he looked at the heirloom. It had been full of magic when Gigi had given it to him, but when she died, the magic had just seemed to die with her. He still kept it with him though, as a talisman of her and his grandfather. Just touching it often made him feel closer to them both.

"Good. It will help you find your way back home," she said with a weak smile.

"Don't worry, Pay. I'm coming back to you, no matter what."

"Promise?"

He hated that there was doubt in her expression, but he couldn't do anything about it other than to prove to her that he was a man of his word. "I promise. And I'll call you every morning before you go into work so we can FaceTime."

She nodded and then chuckled. "We act like you're going to war or something. It's just three and a half weeks. Then you'll be back for a few months before you have to go out again. It'll be okay."

"Are you convincing yourself or me?" he asked her gently.

"Myself," she said. "Maybe a little bit you."

He chuckled softly. "That's my girl."

"You know it." She gently touched his face, gave him one last kiss, and then turned around and left before he was even in the plane.

As her car was leaving the secured area, he sent her a text.

Take care of St. Nick.

When she stopped at a stop sign, she quickly texted back. *Pfft... Like you even needed to ask.*

CHAPTER 27

*a*tlas paced the side of the stage. It was a tour where anything that could go wrong did, and there was nothing he could do to stop it. It was the night before Christmas Eve, and this leg of the tour had been fraught with problems. Sets had failed, and nobody seemed to be able to fix them. One of the opening acts had gotten sick, so Atlas's band had covered for them. The end result was two fried electric guitars, three trips to a healer, two missed FaceTime calls with Payton, and a gash on the forehead.

Nobody was happy. Least of all Atlas.

I don't know why you're so upset. The new songs are rocking our fans to the core. When you finally arrange the tour around them, they'll blow up in the charts.

"Go away, brother," Atlas warned. "I'm not in the mood." Never before had he wanted a leg of a tour to end so badly. For the first time ever, his heart was somewhere else. And he knew where. "I have to make a phone call."

It's not going to change anything.

"We'll see."

Five minutes later, Atlas was on the phone with his manager, Christopher. "How can we get out of this?"

"You can't. Not unless you're up for a legal fight," Christopher said for the third time in the last two weeks. "You can't just cancel shows because you feel like it, Atlas. We've been over this."

"It's not just because I *feel like it*," he shot back. "This isn't safe for us. Already a set fell and knocked one of the backup singers on the head. She had to go get checked for a concussion. I tripped on an unsecured wire and ended up with a gash on my forehead, and now we have a mic spiking with electricity. The venue management has refused to take it out of rotation because they said it's harmless. It's not."

"Just use your own mics," Christopher said, clearly losing his patience.

"We have been using our own mics. That's not the point!"

"I know what you're saying. Someone could get hurt, and that will be tragic if it happens. But for now, the only thing you can do is ride out the contract."

Atlas wanted to reach through the phone and throttle his manager. "I thought you worked for me? That you were supposed to be looking out for me and the band."

"I do. I *am* looking out for you," he insisted. "You're just not seeing it because I'm not giving you the answer you want to hear."

"You know what, Christopher? Why don't you go eff

yourself." Atlas ended the call and then hit his lawyer's number.

"Masterson and Bates," the receptionist said.

"This is Atlas Mazer. Get me Barry Bates. It's urgent."

"Yes, Mr. Mazer. Give me one moment. He'll be with you shortly."

The crowd started screaming, and Atlas knew he had only about a minute before he was due on stage. Luckily, his lawyer came on the line almost immediately.

"Mr. Mazer, what can I do for you today?"

Atlas didn't mince words. "I need you to get me out of this contract. I want to cancel all the rest of the shows through New Year's Eve. And I want you to find just cause to fire Christopher Cain so that I'm not paying him out the nose for the next three years as he rides out his contract. I'm sending you my notes for cause for both actions right now through email. Find something, because this tour isn't safe, and I won't put my band and crew in anymore danger."

"And tonight?" his lawyer asked, making Atlas respect him even more. No one else would have even considered trying to legally get a band out of a contract one minute before a show was supposed to start.

"The band is already on stage, so we'll just do the best we can and pray no one gets electrocuted."

"Do more than pray, Mr. Mazer," his lawyer said. "I don't want anything to happen to my client or his band."

"I'm on it. We'll talk after the show." Atlas ended the call, put in his earpieces, grabbed his personal mic, and ran onto the stage to thunderous applause.

At first, everything seemed great. Hyped fans, energetic band, and a packed setlist.

"Helloooo," he yelled into the microphone. Instantly, he spotted a flash of light near the back of the arena and prayed it wasn't a storm rolling through.

The crowd went crazy in a good way, most of them jumping up and down and screaming Atlas's name. He loved an involved crowd. It just made it more enjoyable for everyone. "Are you ready to rock tonight?"

The resounding *yes* had the band breaking into the intro to their most popular song that wasn't from what Atlas referred to as 'Ashton's emo collection.' Atlas played song after song after song, all of them upbeat and full of life.

When they were about halfway through the set, Atlas pulled the compass out of his pocket and held it up. It was slightly warm to the touch, but there was still no magic clinging to the metal. "This compass was a gift from someone special, and tonight, I want to dedicate the next song to her."

The crowd went wild like he knew they would.

He played a guitar riff and then grinned when he called out the title of Gigi's favorite song, "Love like You Mean It."

The entire venue was alive with energy. The song was a deep cut from an early album and a fan favorite. It hadn't ever been a radio hit, but every time he played it at a show, the fans screamed along word for word as if the song were their personal anthem.

As soon as the chorus started, the entire structure began to shake from the sheer volume of the singing.

Love like you meannnnn it!

Still holding the compass in his left hand, Atlas raised both hands in the air, hyping up the crowd, and that's when he noticed the golden magic sparking from his fist. His first instinct was to stop what he was doing and open the talisman to see what it had to say, but he was in the middle of a fan favorite and was a professional. It would have to wait.

But then a drop of the magic slipped from his hand and landed on the stage to the left of him. It sparked and then faded out, leaving a shadowy figure in its place. He took a step back, not at all sure what was happening, but then he recognized the spirit that was taking form, and he nearly broke down and cried.

Gigi.

It was the first time she'd visited him since she'd passed. Though he hadn't expected to see her since he'd only been visited by Ashton ever since his death. But Gigi had been a medium herself. Maybe that was the difference.

As the last notes to the song faded away, Gigi walked over to him, put her arm around him, and whispered, *It's time.*

"For what?" he asked her.

She glanced up and pointed over their heads. "To move. Do it now, Alistair!"

He caught sight of the swinging spotlight just in time and dove to the side as it came crashing down right where he'd have been standing for his next set.

There was an eerie silence, followed by pure chaos as the crowd collectively processed that Atlas had almost been killed by faulty equipment.

"Atlas, let's go," his lead guitarist said as he tugged him up and off the stage.

The remaining lights had come up, and there was no denying the confusion on the arena floor. The fans were upset, some of them crying. Others were angry. But above all, they were just confused.

Somebody had to say something. But what? Even he didn't know what would happen next. His phone that he'd stuffed in his back pocket started to vibrate. He glanced at the incoming call and answered when he realized it was his lawyer.

"You heard what happened already?" Atlas said.

"We did," Barry said. "Someone here in the office was live-streaming it."

That surprised Atlas. He hadn't pegged his lawyer or his staff as fans. If they weren't, that was even more impressive.

"Okay, so their shoddy equipment almost took me out. Now what?" Atlas asked.

"You've got your cause for canceling the tour. Consider it done, Mr. Mazer, and go enjoy your holidays with your loved ones. We'll take it from here and let you know what we find when it comes to your manager."

"Thank you." He ended the call, looked over at Gigi, who was standing a few feet away, and asked, "Did you do that?"

"Do what?" She winked at him and then disappeared.

He smiled to himself, grabbed a working microphone, and stepped out onto the stage and explained to the fans that due to unsafe conditions, regrettably the show was over.

You can't do this to me, Ashton complained.

"Do what?" Atlas was in his hotel room, packing the last of his things. "Go back to Christmas Grove? Take time off? Figure out what I want out of my life instead of what *you* want out of my life?"

I've never made this all about me! Ashton thundered. *I'm the one who's dead, remember? I go where you go. I'm the one who has to live with your decisions. Meanwhile, I'm the one who feeds you all the hit songs, and without me, you'd be singing in a café somewhere for tips.*

The compass that was in Atlas's front pocket started to grow warm. He was beginning to understand that when there were decisions to be made, that's when the compass woke to help guide him. "There's only one problem, Ashton," Atlas said mildly. "You're not living. You're existing between worlds. Don't you see that? You're trying to live vicariously through me, and it's not fair to me or to you."

You don't know what's fair. You're the one living my dream.

"Because you demanded that I do it, or don't you remember that?"

Ashton paced the room, his spirit becoming more and more agitated by the moment. *What was I supposed to do?*

Now you're asking the right question. Gigi appeared beside Atlas and reached out for Ashton's hand.

Gigi, Ashton said, his tone so soft that Atlas barely heard it. Their hands touched, and that golden thread of magic sparked between them.

I've missed you, my soulful boy, she told Ashton.

Ashton looked like he wanted to cry as he stared down at her comforting face. *I've missed you, too, Gigi.*

Atlas cleared his throat. "I'd leave to give you two some privacy, but I kind of think I might be the person who is tethering both of you to this energy plane."

You are, Gigi said. *Stay. You should hear this anyway.*

Atlas nodded and took a seat at the end of the bed, waiting to see what wisdom Gigi was going to lay at Ashton's feet. It had been over a decade since they'd talked. Atlas imagined it was going to be something big.

He was not disappointed.

If I had to guess, all those tortured love songs you write are about one girl, Gigi said, looking at Ashton.

He nodded even as he glanced away.

And the reason you follow Atlas around is because of two things. You're always hopeful you'll run into her, but you also don't want to sit still because then the thoughts creep in. The ones that tell you you'll never see her again. Or that what you had wasn't real anyway. So you write another brilliant song, and Alistair sings it. The song resonates with anyone who has even half a brain, and then you wait. You wait for her to hear it. To know it's from you.

"And now you're stuck in a cycle, always looking, never finding, and always writing songs that rip your heart out," Atlas supplied. He had a right to speak. He'd been his brother's mouthpiece for too many years to count.

Ashton said nothing as he kept his gaze trained on Gigi.

Their grandmother patted Ashton's ghostly hand and said, *What if I told you she's been waiting for you this whole time?*

Ashton jerked his head up and scanned the hotel room. *Where? She's not here right now, is she?*

She can be. Gigi snapped her fingers, causing the bathroom door to disappear. The opening turned into a gorgeous spiritual world full of color. It also held one other thing.

Ashton's first love.

Chloe, he said, his voice full of reverence.

Ashton? Her eyes were wide with surprise. *Where have you been? I've been waiting for you to find me.*

He didn't hesitate. Ashton hurried into her arms, and the two of them stood there holding each other for what seemed like forever. When they broke apart, Ashton was firmly in the spiritual world and was already starting to fade.

"Wait!" Atlas called. "Is this it? Is this the last time I'll see my brother?"

Not the last, Gigi said. *Someday, after you've lived your life and you're ready to move on, both he and I will be waiting.*

"Not you, too, Gigi," Atlas said, feeling a little panicked and like he was being abandoned. After living his life for years with Ashton over his shoulder, he wasn't sure how he was going to adjust, but he'd damn well try his best.

Not forever. I'll be here when you need me. Like now, when you clearly needed a push to go live your life with Payton. She's worth it, darling. Don't mess it up.

"I won't, Gigi," Atlas promised as she blew him one last kiss and faded back into the ether.

CHAPTER 28

*P*ayton McCabe sat at her dining room table with St. Nick in her lap as she sealed the letter and a check into an envelope. Now all she had to do was find an address. She supposed it was on the contract she'd signed when she agreed to be his fake wife. After pouring a glass of wine, she went to the hutch where she filed all her important paperwork and quickly found what she needed.

She'd thought that once she sent the bulk of the money she'd made on the fake marriage back to Atlas she'd feel freer. Like she'd shed a hundred or so pounds from her shoulders.

She didn't.

All she felt was stupid.

How could she have believed that Atlas Mazer was going to be exclusive with some woman from a small town in northern California when he could be with literally anyone he wanted? People in his circle must've thought she was insane for believing him when he said they were a couple. He'd only called once while he'd been on the road, and even that had been short-lived when he'd been called away to deal with some problem with the band.

That was fine. She understood he had priorities. But after the two weeks they'd shared, she just hadn't expected to be backburnered so easily.

She regretted nothing though. And she knew she'd do it all over again tomorrow, given the choice.

Well, everything except losing Gigi. That she would change. How she'd come to love that woman so much in just four short days was beyond her, but she had. Just like she'd fallen in love with Atlas.

With a sigh, she gave St. Nick a snuggle before getting up to place him in his giant kitty bed. After Gigi had passed, Payton couldn't stand the idea of her beloved kitten going to a stranger. So she'd brought St. Nick home with her, and within a day or two, they'd gotten used to each other. Now Payton was grateful for the little kitty's company.

Once the kitten was tucked into his bed, Payton took the letter to her mailbox. But as soon as she stepped out of her front door, she froze.

Was that really Atlas, or was she just seeing things?

The handsome man she'd fallen in love with was being dropped off in a large black SUV. He had about six suitcases surrounding him, and he was carrying a brown leather bag. When he saw her, his face broke out into the biggest grin she'd ever seen on his handsome face. "Honey, I'm home," he called.

Payton forgot all of her insecurities and ran to him, launching herself into his arms.

He scooped her up and twirled her around, squeezing her so tightly that she found it hard to breathe. But she didn't care. All she wanted was to be in his arms.

When her feet finally hit the ground, she only had a second to catch her breath before he took her mouth and kissed her until she was weak in the knees.

"Whoa, hang on there, gorgeous," Atlas chuckled. "We can't have you collapsing in your front yard because you were starved for my kisses. We'll save that for the bedroom."

She laughed and hugged him again. "Why are you here? How did you get here?" Her eyes narrowed, and her tone sounded like a fifth-grade schoolteacher as she berated him for ghosting her. "And why didn't you make good on those FaceTime calls you promised me? Or even a regular call. For the goddess's sake, Atlas, you could have at least texted!"

"I know," he soothed, running his hand through her hair. "I owe you the biggest apology. All I can say is that the tour was a complete shitshow, one problem after another, and every time I went to call you, another awful thing happened." He pointed to the gash on his forehead. "Like this one. The healer said if she hadn't been available I'd have needed stitches."

"So you were so busy you couldn't call?" she asked, sounding skeptical.

"No. I was so busy and frustrated that I didn't call because I was doing everything in my power to get out of my commitments so that I could come back home to you."

"Home?" she asked. "Whose home?"

"This one," he said, eyeing her pretty yellow house. "Or wherever you want to live. My home is with you, Payton. It doesn't matter to me where the structure is."

Tears filled her eyes, and a lump formed in her throat. "Are you sure? What about your career? What about singing Ashton's songs? I don't want to be the reason you give up music."

"I'm sure. Let's go in so I can tell you all about it," he said and started to steer her toward the house. He'd only taken two steps when he spotted the envelope with his name on it lying on the ground. "What's this?" he asked as he picked it up. "It's not a Dear John letter, is it?"

Payton winced. She must have dropped it when she ran into his arms. "No," she said. "Not exactly."

He raised both eyebrows, looking alarmed. "You'd better explain, because I just upended my entire life to come back here to you. Did I make a mistake?"

"No," she said as she shook her head slowly. "I don't think so. It really isn't a break-up letter, though I suppose you could've interpreted it that way. I was returning the remainder of your money after I paid off the loan on the restaurant. I just felt weird for being paid after everything that happened between us. There's also a payoff schedule to repay every cent, and I asked where I should send your rings. I didn't want to put them in an envelope. They're both way too valuable."

He stared at her, looking dumbfounded. "That sure sounds like a Dear John letter to me."

"I thought you were ghosting me. I didn't expect... this." She waved at his luggage.

"No one would," he said with a laugh. "Come on. I need a stiff drink after all of that. But for the record, both rings are yours, and you can do whatever you want to with the money. A deal's a deal. Keep it, give it away, donate to a charity, open your pie shop. Whatever makes you happy. Just don't try to send it back to me because I'll just refuse."

She rolled her eyes. "You're really stubborn. You know that, right?"

"Only when it comes to you." He kissed her cheek. "Now, where's my Christmas present?"

"Where's mine?" she asked.

He held his arms out wide. "You're looking at it."

She grinned. "You know what? It's just what I wanted. Come on. Yours is on the Christmas tree inside."

"*On* it?"

"Yep."

After they hauled all of Atlas's luggage inside, she tugged him over to her tree that was decorated with her grandmother's glass ornament collection. It was the only thing she'd managed to save from multiple moves and a volatile childhood. They were the pride and joy of her holiday décor.

"See these?" she told Atlas as she handed him his gift. "This is what I've gotten you for Christmas."

"Glass ornaments?" he asked as he tore open the envelope she'd given him.

"Sure. If you want." She gave him a pleased smile.

Atlas looked down at the gift certificate, and when recognition dawned in his gaze, he glanced up at her and said, "This is the best gift I've ever gotten. Thank you, love."

"You're welcome. I can't wait to see what you make."

He chuckled. "Don't get too excited. I seriously doubt I'll be making anything as beautiful as your glass ornament collection during my first six-week class. But I'll give it my best shot."

"Good. But for now, we have other plans," she said playfully as she tugged him in the direction of her bedroom.

"Is that mischief I see in your eyes, Ms. McCabe?" he asked, following her.

"That's not the only thing you're about to see," she said with a wink as she ran into her bedroom, shrieking with delight when he ran after her.

CHAPTER 29

$\mathcal{D}$anny Frost looked around at the people at the opening of his brand-new pottery gallery and finally felt at peace. It had been almost a year since his grandmother Georgia had died. Her passing had ended up having a profound effect on him. She'd always advocated for him to follow his dreams of opening his own pottery studio, and now he had. His parents weren't too thrilled when he quit his corporate job in accounting and told them he was moving to Christmas Grove, but he knew they'd get over it... eventually.

"Danny!" Payton called as she and his cousin, the rock star, Atlas Mazer, made their way over to him. "The shop is gorgeous. I can't believe how fast you got everything up and running."

"Thanks, Payton. I'm pretty pleased with it."

Atlas held out his hand, and when Danny took it, his cousin pulled him in and gave him a quick hug. "She's right.

It looks really great. Your work is fantastic, too," Atlas said. "One day my glass blowing will be just as impressive, but today is not that day," he said with a laugh.

"Oh, I don't know. I've seen a couple of pieces that are quite nice," Danny said, remembering a couple of vases in the cabin on the lake that Payton and Atlas bought together after they made their marriage official down at the courthouse. It was the same one they'd all shared last December before Gigi had passed.

"I've had a few successes," Atlas agreed. "But most are crap. I need a lot more practice. It's hard to do when I'm running around with the band all the time."

"It's not all the time," Payton said. "It's been like six shows." She looked at Danny. "Each one was fantastic by the way. Now that Olivia has a new chef for the inn, I have a lot more time for my pie shop and being a semi groupie for my man."

"I went to one show," Danny said. "You're right, Atlas and his band were incredible. I really like the new songs. I like playing it when I'm throwing pots in the studio. Really fun stuff."

"Thanks, man," Atlas said.

They chatted for a few more minutes until more people started showing up and wanting Danny's attention.

By the time the evening was winding down and Danny was alone in his shop again, he'd sold a sizable portion of his stock on hand and had connected with a couple of people who wanted private lessons. There was no doubt about it; it was a great opening. Right up until he heard the chime on the door and a person he hadn't seen in sixteen years walked in.

"Danny Frost? It that really you? What the hell are you doing in Christmas Grove?"

He gaped at the small fiery redhead with the beautiful violet eyes and blinked, certain that he was seeing things. "Marissa?"

She glared at him.

And that's when he knew his eyes weren't playing tricks on him. He'd just moved to the same town as his ex-wife. The one he'd ghosted right before Christmas when he was just nineteen years old.

"Still no explanation for what went down all those years ago, I see," she said. "Well, good luck with your new gallery. You're gonna need it." Then she turned on her heel and stalked out.

***

Get Danny and Marissa's story in the next book: A Witch For Mr. Garland (Witches of Christmas Grove, Book 6)

For more books in Kindle Unlimited check out these series:
Witches of Keating Hollow
Premonition Pointe
Jade Calhoun

Join Deanna's reader group on Facebook.

To learn about Deanna's new releases sign up for her

newsletter here. Do you prefer text alerts? Text WITCHYBOOKS to 925-722-6086 for news and updates.

Dear Reader, Reviews are always appreciated. Did you love this book? Please take a moment to let others know in the form of a review on your favorite vendor. XOXO, Deanna

DEANNA'S BOOK LIST

Witches of Keating Hollow:
Soul of the Witch
Heart of the Witch
Spirit of the Witch
Dreams of the Witch
Courage of the Witch
Love of the Witch
Power of the Witch
Essence of the Witch
Muse of the Witch
Vision of the Witch
Waking of the Witch
Honor of the Witch
Promise of the Witch
Return of the Witch
Fortune of the Witch

Witches of Keating Hollow: Happily Ever Afters
Gift of the Witch
Wisdom of the Witch

Witches of Befana Bay:
The Witch's Silver Lining
The Witch's Secret Love

Witches of Christmas Grove:
A Witch For Mr. Holiday
A Witch For Mr. Christmas
A Witch For Mr. Winter
A Witch For Mr. Mistletoe
A Witch For Mr. Frost
A Witch For Mr. Garland

Premonition Pointe Novels:
Witching For Grace
Witching For Hope
Witching For Joy
Witching For Clarity
Witching For Moxie
Witching For Kismet

Miss Matched Midlife Dating Agency:
Star-crossed Witch
Honor-bound Witch
Outmatched Witch
Moonstruck Witch
Rainmaker Witch

Jade Calhoun Novels:
Haunted on Bourbon Street
Witches of Bourbon Street
Demons of Bourbon Street
Angels of Bourbon Street
Shadows of Bourbon Street
Incubus of Bourbon Street
Bewitched on Bourbon Street
Hexed on Bourbon Street
Dragons of Bourbon Street

Pyper Rayne Novels:
Spirits, Stilettos, and a Silver Bustier
Spirits, Rock Stars, and a Midnight Chocolate Bar
Spirits, Beignets, and a Bayou Biker Gang
Spirits, Diamonds, and a Drive-thru Daiquiri Stand
Spirits, Spells, and Wedding Bells

Ida May Chronicles:
Witched To Death
Witch, Please
Stop Your Witchin'

Crescent City Fae Novels:
Influential Magic
Irresistible Magic
Intoxicating Magic

Last Witch Standing:
Bewitched by Moonlight

Soulless at Sunset
Bloodlust By Midnight
Bitten At Daybreak

Witch Island Brides:
The Wolf's New Year Bride
The Vampire's Last Dance
The Warlock's Enchanted Kiss
The Shifter's First Bite

Destiny Novels:
Defining Destiny
Accepting Fate

Wolves of the Rising Sun:
Jace
Aiden
Luc
Craved
Silas
Darien
Wren

Black Bear Outlaws:
Cyrus
Chase
Cole

Bayou Springs Alien Mail Order Brides:

Zeke
Gunn
Echo

ABOUT THE AUTHOR

New York Times and USA Today bestselling author, Deanna Chase, is a native Californian, transplanted to the slower paced lifestyle of southeastern Louisiana. When she isn't writing, she is often goofing off with her husband in New Orleans or playing with her two shih tzu dogs. For more information and updates on newest releases visit her website at deannachase.com.

Made in the USA
Monee, IL
16 December 2023